MoonLight Streets

MoonLight Streets

4th Cross

SANJU MURTHY

PARTRIDGE
A Penguin Random House Company

To order additional copies of this book, contact
Partridge India
000 800 10062 62
orders.india@partridgepublishing.com

www.partridgepublishing.com/india

ACKNOWLEDGEMENT

W̲ell, here I'm Sanju Murthy, with my first ever book, end product of our imagination and a story which had been in our minds.

Here I start my note of gratitude for people who had been with us throughout the process of writing this. I place on record my sincere gratitude to my parents Adhi Murthy and Arathi for supporting me all the way, next I thank my best friend Karthik S Kumar and my dear sister Manjushree S S for being with me forever, helping. My special appreciation is for my sister Sharadha Gopalakrishnan who fine tuned our writing skills throughout. I'm grateful to my brother Manjunath and friends Sathya Keerthi, Pragathi, Shikshan, my co-writer Sandeep and my family who had always been a persistent support for me and without whom I would never have discovered the zeal of writing within me.

This is Sandeep Eshaanya, with my first book which was my dream.

I hereby thank my Parents, my dearest brother Santhosh, I also thank my best friend Subhash, Sriram, Praveen Chandra and the Niranthara foundation who are all wonderful and a great source of encouragement. Last but not the least I would like to thank my co-writer Sanju Murthy and the almighty for being together in all my steps.

We thank our college Mahajanas Mysore, where we discovered our imagination boat.

We place on record our deep sense of gratitude to Partridge India Publishers who are a boon for budding writers.

PROLOGUE

I walked alone in the street, overwhelmed. It was pretty cold and I was wearing sweater.

I reached tea house. I went in and sat on one of the table under the bower. I looked at my watch and tapped my feet continuously on the floor. I gazed the street but I didn't find anyone. I was looking forward for the clock to strike ten. It was five minutes to ten when I looked at my watch. It started drizzling when I took my phone out.

Shyam mama brought a cup of tea in a tray. He wished me and I wished him back. He placed the tray on my table.

"Am waiting for someone mama" I said him fervent.

He smiled at me and took back the tray. I stared at street again.

I was delighted when I saw her.

She stood speaking to a pedestrian right in front of tea house.

I stood up looking at her and it brought me the random memories.

I sustained my heavy bag on my shoulder. I walked towards Moonlight streets railway station. It was a bright day, sky was perfectly cloudless blue. I wore my mom's favorite color shirt.

Moonlight Street is the only Kannada speaking area in Ooty city. Ooty has earned a nick name called "The green land", because the whole Ooty is covered with the green mask of tea plantations.

Finally I reached the railway station. There was huge crowd of people, few slept on floor, few were busy walking here and there to buy tickets left out illiterates watched the repeated ads in the television with surprised eyes.

Repeated announcements were made about the arrivals and departures of the trains in three different languages. I rolled my eyes all over the station as I sat on the wooden bench besides dustbin.

I gasped.

I pulled out my reservation ticket and visiting card; I looked at the big clock at the centre of the station to know the time.

"TRAIN NUMBER 56136 IS ARRIVING TO THE PLATFORM NO.6B IN FIVE MINUTES."

The announcement was for my train.

I stood up, took my luggage and walked towards 6th B platform. People started rushing to that platform; I don't have to run for the seat, I said myself looking at my reserved seat number.

Before I confirmed my compartment number train arrived and people started rushing into the train. I waited until the crowd was clear and then got into my compartment. I occupied the seat beside window and kept my luggage aside.

I looked around; all reserved seats were filled except seat number 93 which happens to be my opposite seat. Final announcement was made for our train's departure.

I made my seat comfortable and tried to open the window. I saw a girl in pink Salwar running towards our train, with her luggage in one hand and her hand bag in other, she looked cute in her curly hair and excited face, she combed her hairs back often from her hands.

"She might be 23 years old "I made a wild guess.

"Madam be slow, there is still time for departure" station sweeper implied her in anxiety.

She beamed instead of replying him and got into the train. She entered our compartment and occupied the seat number 93 which was my opposite seat. Soon she dumped her luggage aside, she opened window and shouted-

"Bye Anna I'm going now" at sweeper.

He waved hand in return.

"Funny girl" I said to myself.

Train started moving slowly on the right track and picked up its speed.

We passed by the board that showed, we have come 15 kilometers away from Ooty. I looked at her; she looked cuter this time, playing with her matching pink bangles. She squinted at me often; I noticed but ignored and remained silent.

I observed the pencil sketch half covered in her bag. I turned back to window.

Before I started thinking something,

"Hello" A feminine voice hit my ears.

I turned to her and spotted it was that same girl who said me hello.

"Hi" she wished me again with bewildered eyes.

"Hi" I wished her back.

"Thank God, you aren't dumb" She grinned.

I noticed an emphasized attention in her.

"I have been observing you right from Ooty station, you didn't speak at all, are you a hostile?" She said pulling out a pack of cookie from her bag.

I shook my head.

She offered me a cookie from a pack but I declined.

She shrugged.

"Well I'm Oshini, Oshini Dhavanth" She offered me a handshake.

"I'm Roshan" I gave her a firm handshake.

"Where are you from?" She started inquiring.

I went into the question-"I don't know where I was born, but right now am living in Moonlight streets in Ooty".

Oshini looked puzzled.

"Well, do you really mind if I say I didn't get you?" she said.

"Certain things in life are like that, they aren't clear" I rambled.

She nodded.

I saw a bagful of papers in Oshini's bag. I didn't ask about it instead I smiled at her and she returned the same smile.

"How mysterious relationships are! Minutes back, she was a stranger and now she is an acquaint"

I thought to myself.

I looked at the pencil sketch again.

"Do you want to see the sketch?"

I shook my head smiling.

When Oshini unzipped her bag in search of something, letters fluttered out of her bag in air. Oshini sprinted behind the letters, her excitement mesmerized the passengers.

I helped collecting all papers and packing them back to the bag. We sat back on our seats. After a while she grimaced.

"Oshini are you okay?"

"Okay" she panted after a while.

"You need some water?" I said pulling out the water bottle from my bag.

Oshini received the bottle and emptied half of the bottle, and rubbed the water droplet on her chin.

"What has happened Oshini?" I questioned.

"Yeah, you were right. Certain things in life are like that! They aren't clear" she said, which left me confused.

I couldn't react for a moment; I turned to window, cold air made my face fresh.

"So" She started again.

I focused my look back on Oshini.

"You want to know about those letters right?"

I nodded.

"Love sucked my life" She said in anger.

"Love???" I looked surprised.

Tears rolled down from her eyes.

"Hey" I said on a serious note.

She bent her face.

"Listen, not only you, love suck everyone, even me." I said trying to console her.

It seemed she was consoled by it. Some people feel lighter when they find people with same problem like them.

"Do you mean it? But you don't look like that" She said totally forgetting that she cried a while back.

"I don't look like what?" I questioned.

"Like you had been in a broken relationship, you look decent" she said it in a second.

"Yes I look decent. In fact love made me perfect, look perfect."

"Hmmm interesting"

"What interesting?" I questioned.

"Your love story"

I blinked and smiled.

"After love breaks, people usually get disturbed in life, but how could it make you perfect? Can you please tell your story for me?" She asked me with curious eyes.

Her 'for me' convinced me to tell her my story, since I already listed her from acquaints to friends list, but I refused and said-"No, it's a usual story."

"If you tell me your story, it would help me overcome from my confusions." She tried convincing me.

"Okay listen" I said meekly.

She placed her chin on her palm.

¥ ¥ ¥

16 YEARS AGO IN MYSORE

"Get up lazy fellow, it's time for prayer." Chandan screamed over and over to wake me up.

"Go idiot, I'm not yet done with my sleep" I said pushing Chandan away from me and covered my blanket up to my face.

Chandan started poking me continuously giggling.

"Don't do that Chandu" I screamed.

"Then come out" Chandan requested.

"No, I'm still sleepy."

I heard footsteps coming into our hall from corridor.

"Good morning children" Mother Mercy Paul wished entering our room.

I woke up quickly throwing my blanket aside.

"Are you ready?" She asked.

"Yes Mother we are all ready" I popped.

Chandan gave me an annoyed look.

"Good come to prayer soon" Mother said and went out.

I was still sleepy but I knew I shouldn't oppose Mother Mercy, because she gave everything for all of us in this orphanage.

I rubbed my eyes from my little hands and looked at Chandan.

Chandan held my hand and we started walking to prayer hall. Everybody was there at prayer hall with all the benches filled.

"Where shall we sit now?" I asked Chandan.

"There." He pointed the last empty bench.

I yawned twice. We occupied the last bench. I sat first and Chandan sat next to me.

I placed my head on the desk and snored once to kid Chandan.

"Roshan, don't be an idiot, get up!" Chandan whispered in my ears angrily.

I tilted my head up and sat properly.

"Few people don't know the values of love and peace. Nobody is orphan on this earth; we all are children of Lord Jesus. Children please don't be selfish and jealous, try coming out of those and spread love, peace to the world. Thank you" St. Mary church's pastor Thomas Murphy ended his speech.

We had no sense about those words or speech at that age. We just clapped.

Mother Mercy thanked Murphy and asked other nuns to light up candles in front of crucified Jesus sculpture. Nuns started singing prayer, we followed as usual.

¥ ¥ ¥

I saw an old man in front of orphanage entrance door searching for someone, holding a week old baby in his hand. He was wearing a torn cloth and he had no footwear.

He saw me and Chandan.

"Hey boys come here" he shouted at us.

Me and Chandan looked at each other and went up to him. Baby wailed continuously without a drop of tear in its eyes.

"Who is the owner here?" the old man questioned us.

"Owner? This is not a hostel to own" I argued with him.

Chandan didn't know the difference between hostel and orphanage.

"Okay who is the chief person here?" old man asked again.

"Mother Mercy Paul is everything here" Chandan answered him pointing the big picture of her above the entrance door. He looked at the photo.

"Where can I meet her now?" he asked me.

"Come, I will show you her." I said and took him to the first floor.

Chandan followed us.

"Go in, she is Mother Mercy." I pointed a woman sitting in the big chair, in a cabin.

"Go" I forced him.

He pushed the half closed door and got in; Mother noticed his arrival and got up from the chair with inappropriate expression.

"May I know who you are? And whose baby is it?" Mother started inquiring him.

"I'm Shankarappa; I work for wages as labor in constructions. Today morning I found this baby alone crying in the empty building. I'm poor; I can't take care of this child. So I have brought her here." Old man stopped.

Mother understood and glanced at him from top to bottom.

"What Mother?" Shankarappa asked.

"Nothing, Don't worry about this kid now, we will take care of her" Mother said and called a maid to take the child in.

Mother searched for some papers from the drawer and wrote something on the paper in next three minutes. Mother asked for the thumb impression of the old man below that paper and he did. They spoke for next five minutes smiling and the old man left orphanage after that. Maid smiled at Mother and took the child inside the bathroom.

"Now you can go to your rooms" Mother told us.

Chandan ran towards our room but I stood there gazing at Mercy. She observed my gazing and came down on her knee.

"What Roshan?" she asked me.

"Mother may I ask you a question?" I said looking into her eyes.

"You are still nine years old and you want to question me? Okay what is it?" she asked me laughing.

"If our mothers are ultimate God, why does she leave us in orphanage???" I asked.

Mercy gave me a fake smile puzzled.

"Don't ask mature questions Roshan. Mothers are the first god for all of us. Time and situations lead people to make bad choices sometime." She said and patted my soft cheeks.

I couldn't respond.

"You are too young to understand all these Roshan; you need time to know this world. Now go in and study." She said kissing my forehead.

¥ ¥ ¥

When I opened my eyes in the morning the room was empty.

"They will be in prayer hall, how orthodox these people are? Especially this Chandan," I said myself and got up to fold my blanket.

I kept the blanket and pillow in my cupboard. I walked into prayer hall, to my surprise I found no one in the prayer hall. I wondered where these people have gone. I turned around and looked at crucified Jesus sculpture.

"Who else is not an orphan here, even Jesus is orphan today" I said myself mocking at lonely Jesus sculpture.

I walked near Mother Mercy Paul's chamber and spotted many people surrounded Mother and are repeatedly talking with her.

There were few policemen in the entrance as well. Orphanage staffs and all the children stood behind Mother trying to understand the situation. There were two advocates who repeatedly fired question at Mother. I walked to Chandan and stood behind him. I placed my hand on his shoulder. Chandan felt my touch and turned back, looked at me.

"What is happening?" I whispered.

"I don't know" Chandan shrugged innocently.

I looked at them and tried understanding their conversation.

"Sorry Paul madam. We have sent you a notice five months back stating that government have acquired this land. But we didn't get any reply from your end and now it is mandatory that you need to vacate this place." Senior advocate said showing some files to Mother.

"But how can you do this to an orphanage?" Mother asked the advocate with a sad face.

"This place will be a Mysore airport; moreover this land belongs to government. It is not only you who are vacating. All the people around hundred acres are vacating. Please co-operate with statute." He clarified again.

She remained silent for a moment.

"What should we do now?" she sounded upset.

"No more arguments Mother, vacate the place soon, there is no other way." He raised his voice.

Mother Mercy trembled.

We looked at each other, though we were not aware of the situation.

St. Mary church's pastor Thomas Murphy got down from his car and rushed into the Mercy Paul's cabin.

He wore surplice, Jesus cross and sixties spectacles to his eyes. Advocates and other officers wished Murphy.

He nodded and wished them back. Advocates started showing him relevant documents and spoke in low voice. Thomas checked out all the documents clearly and returned the files to him.

"Mother we cannot recline the law, we should vacate this place" Murphy suggested.

"What are you saying Father? Where should I send these orphan children" Paul said in crestfallen tone.

"That wouldn't be a problem, believe me." Murphy was very confident. He saw Mercy Paul was about to protest but he cut her off.

"Nothing will happen" he assured.

Mercy Paul gave him blank look.

"What???"

"Nothing Father" Mercy agreed to Murphy with a helpless nod.

"We can understand the situation Mother; we are giving you one week of time to vacate. It is in our rule." Advocate interrupted.

"Thank you we will vacate." Thomas Murphy said.

"But make sure you vacate in time, don't make us come here again, we will see you." Advocate said and everyone left.

Thomas Murphy nodded. Everyone got into their vehicles and left. I fixed my look at those vehicles till they disappeared from my sight. Mercy Paul and Father Murphy went inside the cabin and started further conversation. Nuns took all of us to the prayer hall to start that day's prayer.

¥ ¥ ¥

Mercy Paul arranged final dinner for all the orphan children in the orphanage. We all assembled the dining hall sooner than usual time. I wondered seeing Mother Paul herself serving dinner for all of us. I bought two plates from the kitchen. I gave one to Chandu and we sat in the second row.

Mercy Paul skipped chocolate cake for me and said-"I know you hate chocolate cake Roshan."

She knew all likes and dislikes of all the children in orphanage.

I smiled at her.

She served all the dishes. We ate happily. We didn't know the reason behind why Paul called it a final dinner.

"Mother can we go to prayer now?" Chandan asked.

I glared at Chandan.

"There is no prayer today; you all should get up early tomorrow. Go sleep" Mother insisted us.

"Mother there is a huge reply for our advertisement in news paper; we have found enough people who want to adopt our children. And we have also inquired about their backgrounds; I think we can give our children for these selected adopters." Sister Merry spoke continuously showing a list in her hand to Mother.

I looked beside to find Chandu, but he was already left. I ran into our room shouting for Chandan.

¥ ¥ ¥

"Why you always have trouble with lips and nose??? This is not Mother Mercy, try drawing it again" Chandan suggested me, looking at my pencil sketch.

"This is sixth time I'm trying it Chandu, but I'm helpless." I looked again at the sketch trying to re-draw the nose.

Someone snatched the sketch from my hand. I looked up to find who that was.

"Wow!!! Who did it?" Paul asked.

"Roshan, Mother." Chandan replied proudly.

"Nice but why is it incomplete child?" Mother questioned.

"I don't know to draw lips." I admitted my weakness.

"That is you Mother" Chandan said.

"I know, Roshan do you respect me so much?" Mother asked.

I nodded. Her question made me confuse.

"Good, come with me." Mother held my hand and took me out of that room to her cabin. Chandan followed us.

I saw a well dressed Christian woman in her modest dress near Mother's cabin; she stared me and gave me a real smile.

I didn't react.

I stood behind Mother and held her gown tightly.

"Mrs. Jasmine Morris, Here he is! He is the boy I was speaking about, yesterday." Mother pulled me to her front.

"Is it??? He is so cute" The lady pulled my cheeks.

"See Roshan you should be with this lady hereafter, she is your mother now, and she will take care of you." Mother said introducing a complete stranger to me.

I didn't understand her; I just kept staring at Mother.

"Come here child." That lady called me with her extended hands.

I didn't move an inch.

"Go, Roshan" Mother started pushing me, to the lady's arms.

"Why should I go?" I sniffled protesting.

"If you respect me u should go." She insisted me.

Though I didn't understand what was going on, I felt completely insecure with the situation, which brought me a choking sensation.

I blinked and released Mother's gown slowly. Mother signaled orphanage maid to bring my luggage. Chandan was watching all this in disbelief.

"If I had my mother here, she would have not sent me like this. Isn't??" I sobbed.

"Roshan again you are asking matured questions. It's not only you; all other orphans are getting adopted. Even this orphanage will be orphan from tomorrow." Mother Paul said in panic.

I turned back to see Jasmine Morris. She smiled at me.

The remembrance of living my rest of life with Morris brought me a blank feeling.

"Chandan go get ready, you will have to go with someone." Mother Mercy Paul said him.

But Chandan stayed there deeply looking at me.

Maid brought my luggage. Morris took it and kept inside her car.

"Okay then, we will make our move." Morris announced.

Paul came down to me, cupped my face and kissed on my forehead. Morris held my hand and took me near car. I turned back at Paul to convince her for the last time but I failed. We got into car. Every second was killing me. Morris started the car, I opened window to look at Chandan, and I couldn't understand his feelings at that point. His eyes were filled with tears. Paul had a fake smile on her face, which only I could understand. She waved her last bye for me. But Chandan didn't.

Car started moving, tears rolled down my eyes.

¥ ¥ ¥

I started feeling cold and I woke up. I turned my head around to check where I was driven. It was a complete new place for me. I saw blue hills covered with thick smog all around, tall trees, nice roads and complicated curves. People wandered wearing woolen sweaters. I noticed a big board that said "Welcome to Ooty." I rubbed my drowsy eyes; I stared at Jasmine Morris clearly.

She looked at me and smiled.

"Why are you looking at my face?" Her eyebrows reached her forehead.

"Where are you taking me?"

"To our home in Ooty"

"Our home?" I asked again to confirm.

She nodded, concentrating on roads.

When Mrs. Jasmine Morris drove for about twenty minutes, I felt I saw something magnanimous. I opened my window to look out. I was left flabbergasted by the view of a magnificent lamp, surrounded by a well fenced lawn which had benches here and there, where people sat relaxed. Just as I tried coming out of my amazement, Mrs. Morris turned on to a street marked "The MOONLIGHT STREETS." Our car took second cross from the main street and stopped in front of a lavish bungalow.

Jasmine got down and took my luggage out. I got down from the car as well and stretched my hands.

"Tired of a long drive???" Jasmine questioned.

I nodded.

She smiled and went near the door, unlocked the main door and called me in. I looked at the bungalow once, it seemed huge. I went inside; I spotted some photographs on the wall and same old orphanage friend Jesus idle in one corner. I saw luxurious furnitures and some antique displays. Every partition of the house was spacious and had sweet smell.

"See this is your home from today." Jasmine said.

I continued inspecting each corner of the house.

"Are you cold shall I bring you coffee?"

Before I could react for her question, she got up to bring me coffee, but I held her hand. She turned back and came down to me.

"What?" Jasmine asked, expecting a matured question from me.

"Can I know who am I to you?" I inquired.

"I don't know. You have to decide it."

I couldn't decide and just stared her.

"Do you think I can't be your own mother?"

She caressed my hair, she continued "Okay but I think I can replace Mercy Paul's place in your mind."

I didn't speak a word. She touched my hands.

"You are very cold, sit here, I will bring you coffee." she got up and walked inside an open kitchen.

When I sat on the sofa in the living room, I went completely inside the sofa, I liked its cushion, and I stared jumping. It took me in and throwed me up.

After a while Jasmine came back with a tray in her hand. She kept the tray on the table in front of me and poured coffee from the jug to a cup, there were three different kinds of biscuits on the other corner of the tray.

She offered me the coffee cup and said- "Did you like the sofa?"

I sipped coffee and nodded in delight.

"What should I call you?" I asked to confirm.

"Call me Jasmine Morris." She said.

I smiled.

"Finish coffee and take rest, you seem tired." She said.

I looked up to see her face. She held sweater in her hand, waiting for me to finish the coffee. I placed the empty cup on table.

She put me inside the sweater. I felt warm.

"That is your room, come" Jasmine took me upstairs.

I entered into the other luxurious part of the house. I was surprised to see the entire big room, alone for me. Unlike in an orphanage ten of us lived in this kind of a space. I totally enjoyed the house and jumped upon the bed.

Jasmine smiled and left the room.

¥ ¥ ¥

I took nearly one month to get adjusted to the new climate and new person. I spent whole month with Jasmine. She cared me exactly like her own son.

"Roshan what's the date today?" Jasmine asked me.

"Hmm it's May seventh. Why???" I confirmed after seeing calendar.

"Oh!!! Is it seventh! Today I had plans of admitting you to the new school, but we should postpone it."

"Why? What is special today?" I asked in confusion.

"Have you forgotten Roshan? Today is my friend's daughter's birthday"

"Yes Yeah!!! It is at 3rd cross right?"

She nodded. She went to her room, brought a bag and handed me it, which had new clothes in it and told me to be ready at 6 pm.

I took clothes and went into my room, while Jasmine continued cleaning house.

"Roshan…. Roshan are you ready?" Jasmine shouted after a couple of hours.

"Yeah I'm ready." I said looking at the mirror for the last time and ran downstairs.

"Wow!!! You look handsome dear." Jasmine said hugging me.

"Thank you Jasmine." I said not knowing how to address her.

"Come." She held my hand and we started towards Moonlight streets 3rd cross.

As we approached the destination house, Jasmine started advising me-"you should behave very polite there Roshan."

I approved with silence. We entered 3rd cross, I started searching for the birthday girl's house. Then spotted a house well decorated and many lavish vehicles were parked near the house.

Yes I guessed it right; Jasmine took me exactly into that house.

As soon as we entered, someone started hosting us, Jasmine smiled all the way and they started with their conversations.

I focused my look on the guests and the presents all of them had in their hands. Many friends of Jasmine covered and she was busy talking to them. I poked Jasmine in between.

"What???" Jasmine asked.

"Where is the birthday girl???" I questioned.

She rolled her eyes all over the hall in search of birthday girl. It was elusive but still Jasmine indexed the right girl in the middle of the kids' gang.

"Look there she is."

I tried spotting her but failed in the crowd, I started moving front. Jasmine held me back and placed a gift in my hands to present it to the birthday girl. I held it and went towards the crowd. I saw a white short prom dress first, but couldn't see her face. I moved forth, yes, I saw her. She had a clear fair face glittering to the brightness of candles placed on cake. She laughed all the time, playing with her friends, one of the candles on cake said she was eight years old. She had lengthy legs and short hairs. She looked like a queen, like a monarch.

I called her birthday queen in my mind.

I was near her and was staring her. She got my attention and turned to me. I placed the gift in her hand, she extended her hand. Extending hand to receive wishes was practiced for her that day.

I shook her hand and wished her-"Happy birthday."

"She is your new friend in Moonlight streets." Jasmine said placing her hand on her shoulder.

"New friend???" I asked.

"Yes, she is Anvitha Charan." Jasmine introduced.

As soon as that, Anvitha came near me, half hugged and touched her cheeks on mine. I didn't understand that, I stood there blinking my eyes.

Jasmine signaled me to say my name.

"I'm Roshan." I said after Anvitha went back.

I understood Anvitha is from a rich background, she knows that different way of wishing friends like I've seen actresses do in televisions.

Anvitha gave me a big slice of chocolate cake.

I declined.

"Why???" birthday queen questioned.

"I hate chocolate cake." I clarified.

Birthday queen looked at my face in disbelief as if am an alien.

She approved my decline and passed other snacks.

After party I and Jasmine left for home. Jasmine gave me a preamble on Anvitha while going back home.

¥ ¥ ¥

Next morning someone knocked my home front door. I heard banging sound but I didn't care much; I was busy playing video game.

"Roshan look who is that." Jasmine shouted from upstairs.

I dropped video game frowned. I walked near door and unlocked it and opened the door. I looked surprised, it was Anvitha. Before I could say anything, she hugged me wishing in the same style like she did last day.

"Hey birthday Queen" I said in excited voice.

"My birthday is over, I'm just Anvitha Charan now, did you get it teddy bear?" she chuckled.

"Why did you call me teddy?" I laughed.

"Because that was what you presented me in your gift." Saying this she got directly into the living room.

I laughed again loving the way she addressed me, but went behind her talking-"But you look like a queen still."

She really did looked like a queen, the way she dressed in simple black gown, only crown was missing. Jasmine noticed our mocking conversation and called us upstairs. We went up.

"What queen early morning you have turned up to our house?" Jasmine cupped Anvitha's face.

"Aunty even you have started kidding me like your son do." Anvitha said shyly.

I stared Jasmine.

"Shall I take your son out with me?" Anvitha requested.

Jasmine smiled –"He is your friend, you can take him anywhere, but be careful." Jasmine assured.

Anvitha held my wrist. I looked at her face.

"Say bye to your mother." Anvitha suggested.

Jasmine's eyes got wet. She gazed at my face with full of love.

"Bye Jasmine." I said whole heartedly.

Jasmine exclaimed tugging me to hug. I hugged her back emotionally feeling my own mother in her. I came out of her arms after a while. Anvitha and I walked out of the home. Jasmine came near door, waved me bye and shouted to take care of ourselves. I was in deep mother's love for the first time in my life. I relished that moment meanwhile I totally forgot to ask Anvitha, where she was taking me. I resumed and asked Anvitha-"Hey Queen where are you taking me?"

"I don't have enough money to pay my school fees, so I have planned to sell you off." she grinned.

Anvitha's cute smile drew my complete attention at her.

"Am I that expensive?"

"Indeed. You're my expensive gift." Anvitha said and locked my elbow with her hand.

We stopped in front of a laundry shop, in Moonlight Street's first cross. I paid attention to the street's outlook. It was not as beautiful as other three Moonlight streets, there was no much gap between two houses, all houses were small and short, the street was not that tidy, children played in street without much restriction from their parents unlike in our streets, it clearly indicated that poor people lived in that street.

But the laundryman had a better house and clean surrounding compared to the rest of the houses in the street, since his house was at the end of the street.

I saw laundryman came out of his house and started ironing the clothes on the big table under the small shed. I stamped Anvitha's foot and gestured her –"Who is that?"

Anvitha walked up to him. I walked behind.

"You're hiding here?" Anvitha said hitting laundryman's stomach gently.

"Why should I hide kid" He reacted to her punch.

"Then why didn't you drop in for my birthday party?"

"Sorry I had too many clothes yesterday." he apologized.

"You didn't wish me as well, but I didn't forget to bring you cake." Anvitha opened box and offered him the cake. She evinced positive angers on him.

Laundryman received the cake and kept it aside still smiling.

"Don't you like chocolate cake like Roshan?" Anvitha asked

"No, no, all these days I had been alone, but now on I should share everything I get."

"With whom?" Anvitha quizzed in wonder.

"My son" laundryman announced.

"Your son!"

He nodded and shouted to call his son out.

"What Papa." A familiar voice came from inside.

"Come out." Laundryman called out.

A boy of my age came out. I looked at him; I was stunned to see my orphanage best friend Chandan. He looked completely different. He wore simple clothes, holding charcoals in his hands, the black stained his face.

"Chandan……." I shouted with wide eyes and opened mouth.

"Hey Roshan" He shouted back surprised.

Anvitha and laundryman strived to figure out what was happening. I asked about his arrival to Moonlight streets. Chandan summarized everything that happened after I left orphanage.

"Papa adopted me." He said and stopped.

I explained about our friendship in orphanage to them. Laundryman struggled to compose his thoughts.

I looked at Anvitha.

Anvitha remained silent, she still looked gorgeous. Her earrings looked beautiful because of her. I couldn't look aside; I kept gazing at her earrings. Chandan was still happy that we met again.

I gasped.

¥ ¥ ¥

Train cut down its speed moved slower and finally reached next station.

"I was so happy to meet Chandan again." I said and paused.

Oshini released her hand down from her chin, nodding.

"Are you bored of my story?"

"No way, it was quite interesting." Oshini combed her hair back and tied it.

"Your story is relevant to a Kannada movie." Oshini said kidding.

I gave her a bitter look.

"Sorry…" she said with an innocent face.

We stared at each other for a while and broke into laughter at the same time.

I got down from train to bring something to eat, Oshini paid attention at me through window. I bought delicious Mysore masala dose and tea. I came in, passed one plate of dose and a cup of tea to Oshini and I sat back in my seat to eat from my plate.

We started eating without speaking anything.

"Wow, this is my favorite dish ever." Oshini said eating the last piece from her plate.

"So you loved Anvitha, right?" Oshini said in confidence.

"Why? Don't you want to listen further?"

"No… so tell me what happened next?" Oshini requested.

"Finish your tea first."

"Not a problem, please continue." She insisted.

"Okay." I started again.

15 YEARS LATER

"Jasmine…." I screamed stepping downstairs.

I heard the sound of knife chopping something from kitchen.

"Jasmine…" I screamed again, throwing television remote on sofa.

Jasmine came out and leaned against the wall.

"What???" she inquired.

"Don't you care your son???"

"Why not?" She said in an ignored voice.

"Look at Chandan, he is his college's topper, he has convocation program at his college today. He is going to receive honors and appreciation. He had invited everyone except me."

Jasmine sighed.

"Don't you scold Chandan? He hasn't invited your son Jasmine."

"I'm not an idiot to scold such a good boy."

I looked at her face in wonder.

"You weren't there at home when Chandan called our landline five times to invite you; he also said your cell phone was switched off. Moreover why do you expect invitation from your best friend?" Jasmine said and went into kitchen; her statement was filled with anger and perfection along.

I crunched my face and went out of my home.

It was very cold out; I rubbed my hands and got on my bike.

I drove bike to Chandan's house. I parked my bike under laundry shed. I entered Chandan's home.

"Chandan…." I shouted.

"Come in Roshan." Papa called in sick voice.

I went near papa, un-ironed clothes were scattered on mat, papa sat beside them covering blanket and drinking tea for cold. Papa opened blanket to bring me tea, but I declined and made him sit back.

"Papa your son is so arrogant now; he doesn't care me at all."

"My son may be poor, but am sure that he is gentle." he replied moving his gaze to Chandan's photograph on wall.

I nodded keeping my eyes on papa. I noticed lots of love in papa's eyes.

"He is not Chandan's own father but still he is not lesser than his own father." I said myself.

"Who is luckier papa? Is it you or Chandan?"

"Both of us are lucky." papa smiled.

"Okay." I gave a blank look not expecting this answer and shifted my topic.

"But won't you attend this function?"

"I'm not so literate to attend those kinds of programs."

"Okay papa I have to go to his function bye."

I came out and rode towards Chandan's college.

I saw atmosphere of festival in the college, a big arch was decorated with flowers which said M.B.A convocation program. There were many VIP's, few police officers. Students' roamed campus happily, parents were eager to see their children receive degree.

I parked my bike in parking lot and went in; some volunteers showed me the way for auditorium. I walked in that way.

I entered a half filled auditorium thinking there was no one to accompany me, but luckily I found Anvitha. She wore a red mini dress and matching stilettos; she tied her hair back tight. She was fair, tall and beautiful; the posture she sat exactly reminded me a model.

"Hey Queen…" I called out.

Anvitha turned around to spot me. I waved my hand high in air at her and went near her.

"Hey Teddy." she stood up and wished me in her usual style.

We sat next to each other.

"Why are you so late?"

"Even you came off without calling me right?"

"Best friends never wait for invitation." she said in anger.

"Okay okay, calm down Queen, I was just kidding."

Anvitha started smiling. After about thirty minutes, someone started welcome speech.

All the guests got on stage. Later the anchor spoke about the college and said there were twenty toppers in their college. But Chandan topped all of them.

The actual convocation program started, they announced Chandan as the toper and called him up on the stage. There was a huge applause.

I started whistling. Anvitha hit my head and said to keep quiet. Chandan went up on stage, in his convocation dress he looked modest. He received his certificate and honor.

"Mr.Chandan Ram Prasad please speak something for us." anchor requested.

He received mic.

First he thanked his faculty and college for encouraging him. After that I only heard about Papa and Mother Mercy Paul.

I wondered that Chandan still remembered and respected Mother Mercy Paul so much.

"Papa was correct, Chandan is really gentle." I said myself.

Chandan got down and came near us. I stood up and hugged him tightly, congratulating. He thanked and went out of my arms. Anvitha congratulated him as well hugging.

"So can we move now?" Anvitha asked Chandan.

"Just a minute there is a final photograph, I'll be right back." he said and went.

"Okay. We will be in parking lot." I shouted.

Chandan waved hand, gesturing okay. Anvitha and I went out to parking lot. Chandan returned in ten minutes.

Chandan had been to college in Anvitha's car that day, Chandan and Anvitha got into the car, I kick started my bike.

Anvitha started her car.

"Roshan come to Shyam Bendre mama's 'Moonlight Tea House' at 5pm." Chandan said.

I agreed, waved them bye and rode back home.

¥ ¥ ¥

"You are such an idiot Roshan, you scolded him black and blue morning and now you're admiring Chandan." Jasmine said changing television channel.

I was gaffled.

Jasmine brought evening tea, cookies and kept in front of my table.

She sipped tea from her cup.

"Jasmine, Chandan have arranged a small tea party at Shyam Bendre mama's tea house, I'll go there, and I don't want your tea today."

"Tea party?"

"Yes."

"Party is something you do in rare, doing everyday is not party." Jasmine said and took back my cup.

I grinned.

"I'll come home late today, bye." I said and came out.

I walked towards Moonlight Streets 4th cross.

Neither I nor Anvitha will usually bring our vehicles in the evening for Shyam mama's Moonlight tea house.

I entered 4th cross of MOONLIGHT STREETS from one corner, there was a beautiful, well designed empty mansion in this corner but I always thought why nobody lived there.

Moonlight Streets 4th cross was the most beautiful street among all other crosses.

It was clean, perfectly maintained and I always felt like I had been in wonderland when I visit this cross, moreover, the corner mansion adds to the beauty of this cross. At the other end of the 4th cross stayed Shyam mama's tea house, it was another attraction of this cross.

I slowly walked and reached Moonlight Tea House. Anvitha stood out waiting for me; she wore a stylish sweater, jeans shorts and boot to her legs.

As soon as she saw me, she throwed back her straightened hairs. "Teddy what's the time now? You are always late man" she said and stopped speaking for a while and continued "But look at you, how handsome you're looking in this pullover and jeans, you are always my hero teddy, you are the most handsome man in this world." she hugged me and held my elbow from her hands, we walked inside tea house like a couple, I wished Shyam Bendre mama, he smiled in return.

Chandan was already there, he sat on one of the chairs busy texting someone. He equally looked handsome but only one thing that always differ him from me was Chandan always liked wearing decent shirts and pants. He grew up very sensitive and decent.

We went near Chandan. I sat opposite to Chandan, Anvitha sat beside me.

"Shyam mama, three green teas" Chandan shouted.

"Whom are you texting so much?" I asked Chandan.

"I'm not texting, I'm checking mails, and few companies have called me for interview next week."

"Soon Chandu will forget us teddy." Anvitha burst into laughter.

Shyam Deudre mama brought all of our orders and placed on our table.

"Roshan, why is your Queen so happy today?" Shyam mama asked.

"I wish her this happiness in her entire life mama." I said.

Anvitha smiled.

Shyam mama is just a small tea house owner for others but for us he is a good friend.

I took my green tea, Anvitha said- "Only tea? I expected scotch for the party." taking her tea.

"First drink tea, I'll get you scotch in the night." Chandan said and winked at Anvitha, smiling.

"You three friends are three stars of this Moonlight Streets, but one star is missing." Shyam mama announced.

"Not missing mama, yet to come." Anvitha said.

All of us looked at Anvitha.

"Next week one of my childhood family friends will come to Moonlight Streets 4th cross." Anvitha said sipping tea.

Chandan leaned front to listen her properly.

"Yes, they have already bought that corner mansion in 4th cross; whole family will be shifting here next week." Anvitha said.

"To that booth bungalow?" I made my eyes big.

"Shut up Roshan." Anvitha slapped me slightly and smiled.

Chandan kept back his empty tea cup.

Shyam mama took back all empty cups and went in.

¥ ¥ ¥

"Hey, Chandan where is Anvitha?" I saw only Chandan waiting in front of Shyam mama's tea house.

"She is angry on us." Chandan replied.

"Why?"

"Yesterday we had been to trekking for 'dhoddabetta' without informing her right? That is why."

"Oh! Damn" I sighed.

"Mama said she alone waited for us the whole evening in the tea house yesterday." Chandu said.

"She is a girl, how can we take her for trekking at evening, but don't worry I know how to make her smile." I said and took out my phone to text her.

Me: Where are you???

After five minutes.

Anvitha: Why do you want that?

Me: :'(

After three minutes.

Anvitha: At home.

Me: Can you please come near tea house.

Anvitha: No.

Me: I need to speak to you, it's important. Please come here.

Anvitha: Okay, wait for fifteen minutes.

Me: Thank you ☺

"See now I'll make her smile." I said to Chandan.

Exactly after twenty five minutes, I saw Anvitha coming near us. She wore mini shoulder dress but looked very dull. She came, stood in front of me in folded hands and looked aside.

Chandan, me and Anvitha stood under a big tree opposite to tea house.

Neither I nor Chandan spoke a word.

Anvitha stood in the same position for a minute and turned her head towards me.

"What's the matter, why did you call me here?" Anvitha asked in anger.

I looked at her face closely. I swallowed my lump.

"Ann… Anvitha" I took much time to call her name.

She gasped closing her eyes and said-"What?"

"I wanted to say you this long back but…" I stopped.

"Say me what?" she muttered.

I went close to her, looked in her eyes deeply and sat on my knee, held her hand.

"I love you madly Anvitha, please accept my proposal." I said, stood up quickly and hugged her.

Chandan burst into laughter.

She pushed me away laughing out loud and said- "Teddy, this is the 8th time you're proposing me. This has been your trick to make me smile, isn't?"

"But consider my proposal Queen." I said still in a funny mood.

"Shut up Teddy." Anvitha said with a big smile and held my hand.

"Look I'm the only man, who can bring that magical smile on your lips, when you are in your heights of anger."

"Honestly Teddy, that is so true. You are my best friend ever; I want you and Chandan all my life like this."

"You will be my Queen even if I get my girl friend one day." I said holding her hand.

Anvitha hugged me.

"Guys what about me?" Chandan cheered.

We let him space, Chandan joined us. Three of us hugged emotionally, Chandan and Anvitha's eyes filled with tears.

¥ ¥ ¥

I got up a bit early that day. I checked my phone; there was no notification for me.

Neither Anvitha nor Chandan ping me. Later I realized that Chandan was busy with some interviews and Anvitha was busy joining for modeling school.

Yes, Anvitha met me and Chandan a couple of days back to ask our opinion on her joining for modeling school. Both of us agreed happily, since we knew that she suits that profession perfectly. I went out to my terrace, stretched my arms and observed 2nd cross from there. There was a huge smog fall that day. People wandered wearing sweaters to avoid severe cold. I turned back to get in but heard a melodious voice shouting-"I love this climate Amma."

I looked back at the road again. I spotted a girl in blue langha dhavani (a traditional dress for an unmarried girl in Karnataka) who held her long plain skirt a bit up to avoid its border touching the road, giving a huge smile looking up. It clearly indicated that she was enjoying the smog fall.

"But we should go for the 4th cross, this is 2nd cross Apoorva." A woman in sari near her said pulling her hand.

"Okay Amma." she said and started moving away from my sight.

I ran downstairs quickly and went out of my house without changing my sweater and shorts. Jasmine saw me rushing and came up to door.

"Where are you going Roshan, its freezing out, come in" Jasmine shouted.

I ignored and started following the girl. Now I had a clear look at her. She wore jumki to her ears, her hands were full of blue bangles, and she had a long tied hair and had perfect shape. She looked like a beautiful, typical Kannada girl. When she carefully kept every steps her ankle bracelets sound made my heart melt. I was totally hypnotized for her beauty. Her deep brown eyes and that cute smile on lips made her look like a full moon.

Yes, it was perfectly like a real white moon with a blue background walked on Moonlight Streets. By the time I got my sense, she ran into the 'corner mansion' at 4th cross. I was fascinated to see this girl getting into that bungalow.

I stood there still stunned for the way she carried herself.

I noticed a man in his fifty years of age gazing at me in suspicious from that bungalow. To avoid the awkwardness, I walked towards Shyam mama's tea house.

I was disappointed to see 'tea house' still closed.

"Why mama hasn't opened his 'tea house' yet?" I asked myself confused.

I stepped back home.

¥ ¥ ¥

When I woke up it was already 4pm. I unplugged my phone from charge. I saw three missed calls from Chandan and five messages from Anvitha. All messages asked me the same question that where I was? I walked down and called Jasmine.

"Yes Roshan." I heard her voice from the garden, I went near her.

Jasmine was busy trimming a rose plant.

"Jasmine am hungry get me tea and something to eat."

"Tea? Won't you go to tea house today?"

"Shyam mama has not opened his tea house today."

"Why?"

"Who knows?"

"Go to his house and check what's wrong."

I beamed at her.

Her eyebrows reached her forehead asking me what.

"What makes you care everyone?" I asked.

"Because Jesus cares me and to return that care on others is my duty." She said.

I smiled and kissed her forehead.

"Okay, come get me something to eat, I have to go to Anvitha's place."

She placed her arm around my shoulder and we walked in.

Jasmine entered kitchen. I walked up to my room to get ready. I dressed up with black shirt and light blue jeans, I ensured in mirror whether my spike was perfect.

I went downstairs. Jasmine sat on dining table waiting for me with upma in a plate and tea beside. I sat on chair and started eating upma. Jasmine kept staring me. I caught her and asked what.

"You are very handsome Roshan." she said smiling.

"Thank you Jasmine." I said with huge love.

I got Chandan's call, I received it. Chandan called me to Anvitha's house immediately.

I agreed and disconnected his call. I finished eating upma and denude tea cup. I said bye to Jasmine and took out my bike. When I came out on road, my mind reminded me that Kannada girl, whom I saw morning. I was so taken away for her beauty and innocent face. I scratched my head, smiled myself.

I wore goggles and rode to 3rd cross.

I entered Anvitha's house, spotted more than three pairs of foot-wears outside. I stood there and leaned my body inside the main door and looked every corner. I noticed the same girl sitting on sofa in-between a woman and a man.

I was surprised and thrilled. Anvitha's mom noticed me and called me in.

Everyone in the living room focused their looks on me as I walked up to the sofa Chandan and Anvitha sat on and I stood behind them.

"These three are thick friends, right from their childhood." Anvitha's father said pointing me, Chandan and Anvitha.

"Everyone in Moonlight Streets knew they are very close friends." Pushpa aunty (Anvitha's mom) said to the uncle and aunt, who sat besides that Kannada girl.

Pushpa aunty also introduced the uncle sitting next to the girl.

"Hi uncle, I'm Roshan" I stretched my hand.

"Hi Roshan, I'm Ramesh" uncle shook my hand.

"This is my wife Radha Ramesh" he said pointing to the aunty next to that girl, he continued-"And she is my daughter Apoorva." he said holding that girls shoulder in his hand.

The moment he introduced her to me, my heart started beating rapidly, I was completely nervous for the first time in front of a girl.

"Hi, Hi Apoorva I'm Roshan" I extended my hand to her.

But she wished me back folding her hands just below her chin in a traditional way. Chandan burst into laughter, Anvitha followed him. I withdrew my hand back humiliated. I gave a fake smile and shifted the topic.

"Hey Queen am going to Shyam Bendre mama's house, will you come with me?" I asked.

"But why Teddy?" Anvitha questioned.

"He has not opened his 'tea house' from morning, I think something is wrong." I said.

"Why didn't you say this before?" Chandan asked.

"Because you guys are so busy, that is why."

"Roshan why do you fail to understand us every time" Chandan said in apathy since he was very sensitive, he takes everything very serious.

"Idiots stop this stupid conversation" Anvitha hit both of us on head and held our hands.

We slammed our mouths.

"So come we will go" Anvitha said pushing me and Chandan towards door.

"Excuse me, can I accompany you guys?" Apoorva asked in soft tone.

I looked apart not interested in her accompanying us.

"You? With us?" Chandan dragged.

"Yes, don't you accept me as your friend?" She smiled.

"Hey, no, no, in fact we all are happy to have your company" Chandan replied.

"Guys please come soon" I said in a harsh tone.

Apoorva gave a weird look.

¥ ¥ ¥

I and Anvitha walked ahead of Apoorva and Chandan.

"Teddy, do you know the address?"

"Yes Queen, his house is in Havelock hills."

Apoorva and Chandan were busy speaking. Both of them are of same wavelength so they got along soon.

We finally reached Havelock hills, it was out skirts of Ooty, and the area was not developed.

"This is Shyam mama's house I guess." Anvitha said.

"Silly, Shyam mama's house is smaller than this and his house is cement in color." I said.

We walked for another three minutes and reached Shyam mama's house. His house was very small, the door was opened. I pushed it to indicate my arrival and we went in.

"Oh Roshan, come in." Shyam mama said trying to get up from his cot.

"Sleep mama no problem, don't strain yourself." Chandan said.

Anvitha came down on her knee; she put her palm on Shyam mama's forehead to check fever level.

"Nothing serious Anvitha, just a usual fever" Shyam mama said.

"Take care mama" Chandan said.

Apoorva stood behind looking at all of us.

"Who is this girl?" Shyam mama asked pointing to Apoorva.

"She is my childhood family friend mama, the other day I said you right" Anvitha explained.

"She is the new star of our Moonlight Streets" Chandan exclaimed.

"No you're wrong Chandan, she is the original moon" Shyam mama said smiling.

Apoorva blushed, Chandan was excited. Even if it seemed true, it irritated me. Anvitha stood smiling.

¥ ¥ ¥

"Roshan is jealous of you right?" Apoorva sipped green tea and looked at Chandan.

"On me?" Chandan kept his cup on table.

"Yes" Apoorva said pulling her black langha with orange border, which Chandan stamped.

She looked beautiful in black langha and orange dhavani.

"Oh sorry" Chandan said taking back his leg.

"Why do you think he is jealous on me?" Chandan asked.

"I don't know whether it's jealousy or something else, but I observed lots of negativity in his conversations with you." Apoorva said.

"I don't think so, he is a very good person, and moreover he is my best friend right from my orphanage days."

"Orphanage …!" Apoorva was shocked.

Chandan sipped tea and nodded.

"What are you saying Chandan? What is this orphanage is all about?" Apoorva's face was sympathetic.

"Yes!!! Caring hands orphanage, it is in Mysore."

"Why both of you were there???"

"Because that is the place where orphans should be" Chandan's voice was low when he said it and his eyes filled with tears.

"Hey Chandan" Apoorva said on a serious note.

Chandan bent his head down.

"To be honest, you and Roshan are so lucky to be orphans" Apoorva said and her face turned dull.

"Lucky? For what?" Chandan looked up at Apoorva.

"You were just born orphans, today you have everyone. But I was born in a joint family, but we have no one today" Apoorva was stuck in her deep thoughts.

Chandan gave a startled look at Apoorva. She wiped her tears, gave out a panic breath and looked aside. Chandan was puzzled for a moment but still he resumed his talk-"Apoorva can I know what happened?"

"Just leave it" Apoorva stood up to leave.

"You don't like sharing things with an orphan right? After all I'm an orphan."

Apoorva looked at Chandan in her red eyes.

"Chandan don't dare speak like that again." Apoorva blustered.

Chandan looked at her empty cup at the other end of the table. Apoorva went back to her seat.

"I don't know what you people have thought of me, but I really have a very good friendship with you, I promise."

"Am sorry" Chandan blithered.

Apoorva gasped, closed her eyes to remember her past. She opened her eyes after a while.

"Have you heard about Upadhyais software?"

"No" Chandan shook his head.

"Well, it is in Nanjangud, which is our native. The company belongs to our family; we had quite a good name. My uncle Suresh was one of the partners with my dad and He was my dad's younger brother, after his marriage, my dad gave him the entire authority of the company. My dad had lots of hopes on him, we all loved him so much, but he started cheating on us. Year on year our company's profit went down. One fine day my uncle eloped with his son and wife, all well settled to Singapore.

All share holders started demanding back their money. My uncle was a sly, he took maximum assets of the company with him. My dad finally sold out everything we had along with the company to repay the debts.

After all these me and my parents were fed up of Nanjangud life. Anvitha's dad and my dad were friends from their college, he stood behind us helping throughout this incident, later when my dad said him that he doesn't like living in Nanjangud, it is he who again helped us buying this corner mansion in Moonlight Streets." Apoorva finished saying dejected.

"You don't have any properties now?"

"As far as I know, we don't have any properties except this mansion but few days back my father said we also have a small school, but I don't know where it is."

"Yes you are right am lucky; I don't have any relatives to cheat me" Chandan said.

Apoorva nodded smiling bitterly.

"I don't know who my parents are, I grew up at 'caring hands', Mercy Paul looked after all of us really well. God gave papa as my father, I met my friend Roshan again here in Moonlight streets, friend like Anvitha is the greatest gift and now you are an addition for all these.

You all are not my blood relatives but I don't think I would have been this happy, if I had any relatives, I hate blood relationship after hearing your story" Chandan said rigidly.

Apoorva gave him a pleasant smile. Chandan smiled back, like he imitated her.

"Sorry am a bit late" Anvitha said beating Chandan's head.

"Not a bit, you're too late" Chandan said himself hugging Anvitha.

"Where is Roshan?" Chandan asked.

"He is busy with his Company secretary exams." Anvitha said and sat beside Apoorva.

¥ ¥ ¥

"Next month I've my Company secretary exams, I've not seen my friends since a week. They know about my busy schedule." I said myself opening my text books.

From past two weeks reading has become my only hobby. C.S is one of the toughest courses, like few other courses. I usually switch off my cell phone, when I start studies. I heard Jasmine calling out my name. I opened my room door and asked her what.

"Anvitha's call for you" Jasmine held landline receiver.

I went down and received receiver from Jasmine.

"Hey Queen, how are you?"

"I'm good Teddy, how is your studies?"

"Good" I smiled.

"Teddy can you do me a favor" Before I could reply, she continued-"I have practice of fashion show a bit early today, can you drop me near my modeling school?"

"That's not a big favor Queen, be ready, I'll be there in twenty minutes."

"Okay, thank you teddy" she kissed me over phone and hanged phone.

I finished taking bath in ten minutes and got dressed in sweater and jeans. I took my bike out of compound, I remembered Apoorva. So I decided to reach 3rd cross, after visiting 4th cross. I rode in front of corner mansion. Apoorva stood out in garden, was busy on phone. She wore white plain langha dhavani. She looked cute like any other day. She spotted me riding and raised her arm and smiled. I returned her the same smile and rode back to 3rd cross via tea house. I had started hating Apoorva's attitude after the incident, where she insulted me folding her hands instead of handshake.

I reached Anvitha's home, I called out her name. Pushpa aunty came out and called me in.

"No aunty, its already late for Anvitha." I declined going in.

Anvitha was in hurry; she wore her brown sandals and rushed towards me. She was dressed in black pencil pant, brown t-shirt, a stylish brown shawl and ponytailed her hair, she looked hot. She hugged and kissed me, I hugged back her.

"Teddy it's getting late." Anvitha said and got on my bike.

"Bye Amma." she shouted at Pushpa aunty.

I took twenty minutes to reach her modeling school and stopped my bike in front of the school. Anvitha got down.

"Teddy do you know something?" Anvitha popped.

"What's new Queen?" I was eager.

"Next week there is 'femina miss Ooty' and am contesting in it." Anvitha jumped.

"Wow you will definitely rock Queen" I said haughtily.

"Thank you teddy, but keep it secret huh!!! Will give everyone a surprise!" Anvitha warned and winked.

I gave her an Indian headshake.

"Okay, its late bye" Anvitha hugged me and walked towards school.

I stood there still looking at my Queen. She entered her school gate, her friends covered her. Anvitha made some space and turned back, waved her hand at me. I waved back. Her smiling face reminded me of our first introduction evening.

"Am so lucky to meet Anvitha in my life" I said and smiled myself.

¥ ¥ ¥

Chandan was amazed. He stared Apoorva in his door with goggle eyes. It was first time ever Apoorva visited Chandan's house. Chandan always liked the way Apoorva dresses because she never wear anything else except, some different colors of plain langha dhavanis, long golden jumkis and matching bangles.

She looked gorgeous in plain red langha dhavani with golden border that day.

"Hey Apoorva! what a surprise?" Chandan cheered.

Apoorva smiled and went inside. But Chandan's excitement made her smile again and again. Chandan's house was small and short, but it didn't bother Apoorva. She never looked anywhere, she focused whole of her sight on Chandan's face. Chandan brought a retired wooden chair and asked Apoorva to sit.

"That's okay Chandan" Apoorva refused politely.

Apoorva rolled her eyes on Chandan's graduation photo on wall, an old cycle and some sports cups.

"Your home is quite interesting." She said.

"Does it look like an exhibition?" Chandan started laughing.

Papa entered home with a sick cough. Chandan stopped laughing and stood up straight with a serious face. Apoorva stopped smiling and whispered- "Who is this?" in Chandan's ears.

"Papa" Chandan whispered her back.

"Chandan iron these clothes, when you are free" papa handed a bagful of clothes to Chandan.

Chandan received the bag with a nod.

"Who is this?" papa pointed his finger towards Apoorva.

"She is Apoorva papa, that corner mansion girl of 4th cross."

"Oh… this is the girl you were telling about a few weeks back?" papa gave Apoorva fondling look, smiling.

Apoorva wished papa folding her hands. Papa returned her wish meekly in the same way. Papa took a bag of ironed clothes and went out to return it to the houses it belonged.

"How gentle he is" Apoorva said and gasped.

Chandan chuckled out.

"Okay, I forgot to ask you this!" she hesitated a while and continued- "Chandan, would you mind spending this whole day with me?"

"Me? With you?" Chandan said titillated.

"Yeah, who else?"

"Okay, I will come." Chandan assured.

"Thank you" Apoorva said with a big smile.

"If you don't mind can you wait for me out for a while, so that, I can change my dress. There is no separate room here." Chandan said embarrassed.

Apoorva giggled and went out. Chandan came out after ten minutes, well dressed in full arm red shirt and blue jeans.

"Oh… we are matching each other today" Apoorva said looking at Chandan's red shirt and continued-"And you are looking handsome." She smiled.

Chandan was stuck for a while thinking something.

"Shall we move?" Apoorva pointed at her Honda active.

"Me and you on the same bike?" Chandan looked innocent.

"I know you are a gentleman, but no problem, come sit."

Chandan got on her vehicle, Apoorva started riding. They conversed all the way, not letting boredom a space. After about an hour of riding, they reached outskirts of Ooty. Apoorva stopped her vehicle in front of a building, which was boarded on the top "ALL INDIA SPEECH AND HEARING CENTRE."

"Where have we reached?" Chandan questioned, getting down from vehicle.

"AISHC" Apoorva said locking her vehicle and they walked towards the building

Chandan saw plenty of small children, while walking inside, children were striving to converse with actions, they were all silent.

"Apoorva, what has happened to these children?"

"They are all dumb and few are blinds." Apoorva said plaintive.

A lady of age about twenty four, started hosting Apoorva, Chandan lagged back. He looked at the name badge on the lady's white blazer and understood she was Dr. Parinitha. She took Apoorva and Chandan into the AISHC Dean's chamber. Apoorva and Chandan sat on the adjacent chairs, opposite to Dean; Parinitha stood beside Dean's chair and whispered something in Dean's ear.

"Hello Ms Apoorva, how are you doing?" Dean wished her.

"Am good doctor, thank you and meet my friend Chandan Ram Prasad" Apoorva pointed at Chandan.

While Chandan shook his hands with Dean, Apoorva continued-"He is an M.B.A topper."

"Oh… nice to shake hands with a topper" Dean laughed.

Apoorva, Parinitha and Chandan laughed as well. Apoorva pulled out an Rs1, 50,000 cheque from her bag, signed it and pushed it towards the Dean gently. Dr. Parinitha received the cheque.

"Thank you for your donation" Dean said and smiled.

Apoorva and Chandan stood up.

"That's my pleasure, but please make use of this money sir" Apoorva requested.

"Definitely we will" Dean answered her.

Apoorva announced their departure. Chandan shook Dean's hand. Apoorva walked out of chamber, Chandan followed her.

"Look at that small girl, within few months, she will be able to see world like us." Apoorva said pointing to a blind girl playing.

"What's going on? Am confused" Chandan said while they reached their vehicle.

"I have habit of donating small amounts every year, to these kinds of trusts or orphanages Chandan" Apoorva smiled.

"Hmm… Apoorva, you have really done a great job."

"There is nothing great in it" Apoorva said and sat on her vehicle. Chandan sat behind her, he smiled.

"She has a good attitude and great heart along" Chandan said himself and chuckled out.

¥ ¥ ¥

"Hello" Anvitha said on phone.

"Hey Queen! What's up? Didn't sleep huh?"

"No teddy I'm practicing ramp walk in my room."

"What time is the show tomorrow?"

"It starts at 8pm."

"Okay, have you said about this to anyone?"

"No, it should be a surprise teddy. I have told my parents that I will be going for my friend's fashion show, I have also invited them. They will be ready at 6:30. Pick my parents, Jasmine aunty, Apoorva and Chandu in our car and drive them to show. Make sure you be there in time, got it?"

"Okay, you don't worry about it."

"Okay teddy bye good night, take care."

"Bye Queen take care"

Next evening, I took an 8 seated Duster car out of car shed from Anvitha's house. Jasmine and Anvitha's parents occupied back seats. Chandan occupied the seat beside me in front.

"Where is Apoorva?" I questioned Chandan.

"She said that she can't turn up to show" Chandan replied.

"Where is Anvitha?" Chandan questioned me back.

"She is already there to accompany her friend." I said and started driving towards the venue.

I reached the show's venue at 8pm, I parked car in parking lot. We all got down from car and rushed in. I saw a big stage well decorated and written "FEMINA MISS OOTY" on it.

We all had VIP passes but still we didn't get seats in front row, we occupied 10th row.

"Where is Anvitha?" Pushpa aunty asked me.

"Might be speaking to her friend backstage, she may come in minutes" I stuttered.

I opened my phone and texted Anvitha.

Me: We all are here.

Anvitha: Oh nice, but am feeling a bit nervous teddy ☹

Me: Don't be, you will definitely take away this crown.

Anvitha: Hope so.

Me: All the best Queen. Will be waiting to see you on stage.

Anvitha: Thank you; Keep watching I'll fascinate you all ;P

Me: For sure you will. Bye.

Anvitha: Bye ☺

Meanwhile anchor had introduced three judges of the show. 1st lady was an established model, 2nd woman was a famous fashion designer and the last person was a young successful businessmen. He further said that there are fourteen girls competing to take away three crowns.

The best smile, the best runway and the big Miss Ooty awards for which we didn't pay attention. Judges sat on their seats; we didn't have a clear look on their faces. Anchor left the stage.

Different color lights started dancing on stage, music bounced out loud, girls started hitting the stage wearing different kinds of designed and colored gown's, they all walked through ramp one after one and disappeared. I was waiting for Anvitha. After 13th girl, lights went off for a second and all of a sudden there was a bright silver light on Anvitha's face.

She stood in the middle of the stage in rich Fuchsia gown, she had the highest heels, she had ever wore to her legs and looked like a magnificent doll. Anvitha's parents, Jasmine and Chandu were surprised to see Anvitha on stage. They were happy and started clapping. Anvitha held her gown a bit up and started cat walking to hit the head ramp.

She walked in an elegant facial expression, she walked exactly to the rhythm of the music, she walked like the whole town was her kingdom, and she walked like she never cared her denizens. She stood on the edge of the ramp giving an elegant pose.

Judges were mesmerized, people were driven crazy. They clapped, Whistled and cheered her. Pushpa aunt's eyes turned into happy tears. Chandan leaned towards me and shouted-"she is worth to be called a Queen."

I smiled nodding.

After three seconds of posing, Anvitha turned back and went off. Anchor asked judges to announce and give away the crowns. All the judges got on stage, each judges announced girl number four and nine as the best smile and best run way respectively.

Before announcing Miss Ooty, people started shouting girl number 14 repeatedly.

The young businessman announced Anvitha as Miss Ooty and put crown on Anvitha.

Anvitha held his hand and walked on ramp again. We all stood up and clapped happily.

Thirty minutes later Anvitha came to us in changed dress. I and Chandu hugged her congratulating. Jasmine and Anvitha's parents looked proud.

¥ ¥ ¥

"Why didn't you attend Anvitha's fashion show?" Chandan sipped green tea.

"I didn't know she was contesting." Apoorva pulled tea cup near her.

"At least did you congratulate her?"

"No, I will call her in the evening."

"What kind of a friend you are!" Chandan bantered.

Apoorva stared Chandan piqued.

"Sorry" Chandan said and stood up.

Apoorva smiled gesturing Chandan was excused. Chandan paid the bill.

"Bye mama" Apoorva waved.

"Bye Apoorva" Shyam mama waved back.

Apoorva and Chandan walked towards the corner mansion.

"So how did Anvitha performed?"

"She was awesome on stage, she looked like a Queen" Chandan exclaimed.

"I know she has that virtue. Roshan rightly calls her the Queen." She said.

Chandan smiled.

"But I missed my best friend's show." Apoorva crunched her face.

"It has all started just now; she has a long way to go. Don't be disquieted, you can see her time and again on stage from here on." Chandan convinced.

Apoorva smiled.

Meanwhile they reached the mansion, stood in front of gate and continued their conversation.

"So what about your interviews?" Apoorva asked Chandan.

"I've given a couple of interviews but still waiting for replies."

"Don't worry Chandan Companies will be in queue to hire you." Apoorva said and winked.

"Are you joking?" Chandan laughed.

Anvitha was on her way home from college, in her car. She noticed Chandan and Apoorva, who were mesmerized with laughter and didn't see the world pass by. Since Anvitha was hurrying home, she didn't stop to wish them. She drove home.

¥ ¥ ¥

Finally my C.S exams got over. That morning, I had nothing much to do. It had been weeks, since I met my friends, I planned to visit Anvitha's house. I walked to 3rd cross I opened the gate of Anvitha's house and went in.

"Come sit Roshan, how is Jasmine doing?" Pushpa aunty hosted me.

"Jasmine is fine aunty, where is Queen?"

"She is in her room Roshan." Pushpa aunty said and went into the kitchen.

I walked up to her room and pushed the door.

"Hey teddy bear" Anvitha called turning to me.

I walked and sat next to her.

"How did exams go?" She asked, doing something on her laptop.

"It was good" I replied, "Have you met Chandan since a week?"

"No, I have not met him, but I saw him with Apoorva last week. They are pretty busy with each other teddy".

"Is it???" I asked with goggled eyes.

Anvitha nodded.

It didn't seem like it bothered her as much as that did on me. I acted all the way normal, but deep inside me, it pinned my heart without telling me the perfect reason.

"Damn, why should I even care about her? She is simple, am stylish, she has loads of arrogance too. We don't match. I hate her, I hate her." I said myself over and over.

Anvitha gabbed my head from her hand and brought back me to the world.

I focused my sight on her laptop. She logged on to her profile.

"You're looking gorgeous." There was a comment for Anvitha's picture. I looked at Anvitha, she understood my questioning look.

"Shravan Rao, Do you remember he was one of the judges at femina miss Ooty. He was the judge, who crowned me." Anvitha said beaming.

"Oh… The businessman, I can't make out him; we didn't see him from close enough to recognize him." I said recalling.

Anvitha nodded.

Later Anvitha suggested a small walk. I agreed to it with a smile. She turned her laptop off, pulled a shawl from her closet, I stood up. We were out of her house and we walked to 'Tea house'.

"Teddy shall I call Chandan and Apoorva too to tea house?"

Looking at my silence she didn't drag the topic. We almost reached tea house at 4th cross.

"Teddy, look who is sitting there!!!" Anvitha said in wonder.

I looked in the direction of Anvitha's pointing finger. Chandan and Apoorva sat next to each other, under the bower and sipped tea laughing, smiling, cracking jokes.

I was jealous deep inside, we moved up to them. Chandan noticed us from distance; he finished his tea and placed his empty cup on the wooden table. Apoorva hosted, wishing Anvitha and smiling at me. Chandan stood up and sat beside me, Anvitha occupied his seat, which was opposite to me and thanked Chandan. Chandan smiled in return.

"What Chandu, you are sooooo busy with Apoorva these days?" Anvitha said.

I placed my left hand on his shoulder.

"Nothing of that sort, you people were busy with your private works, meanwhile, I spent my time with Apoorva and am happy that the time spent with her turned precious." Chandan said and looked into Apoorva's eyes.

"Oh!!! Apoorva is put on cloud nine now." Anvitha uplifted her voice.

Apoorva's eyes met Chandan's; she put her head down smiling at Anvitha's comment. Anvitha stood up and pulled Apoorva out of the chair to go inside the tea house to order teas. While they were walking inside they whispered something in ears and kept laughing. Chandan placed his hand on mine, I looked at him.

"Roshan, I should say you something." Chandan breathed.

"Yes" I nodded coming out of the jealousy that I had on them.

"You know, I think I like Apoorva." Chandan stuttered.

This instigated me to fool him.

"Chandu, you just like her now but I'm already in love with her from the day I saw her." I mislead him.

He looked at me stilled like a storm passed all over him.

"Really???" Chandan asked in a squeaked tone. I nodded again with a fake smile. He slammed his mouth; I noticed a bundle of sadness in his face. That moment give me an infinite fun. I turned my face aside and giggled lightly. I sat back straight again.

"How beautiful she is! I had no clue of an angel until I met Apoorva. I always want Apoorva to be my angel." I said in closed eyes.

Chandan looked at me again in plunged face and he gulped. I threw him frequent smiles to ensure my acting looked real. Meanwhile Apoorva and Anvitha came back to their seats.

"It had been a month and a half almost since I talked to mama, today I spoke enough." Anvitha said to Apoorva and smiled.

Shyam Mama brought four cups of tea in a tray and placed them on our table. He observed Chandan's sluggish face.

"I don't want tea." Chandan pushed his cup slightly aside.

"Why Chandan? What's wrong?" Shyam mama asked Chandan.

"Nothing mama, before they arrived, I already had tea once." Chandan said digesting his sorrows.

"I think something is wrong" Shyam mama said taking back Chandan's cup to his tray.

Chandan shook his head; Apoorva and Anvitha were still busy gossiping about something. I went near Shyam mama.

"Something is there, I will tell you later" I whispered in his ears.

Shyam mama nodded and went back into the tea house.

Apoorva glanced at Chandan's face steadily and lifted her eyebrows. Chandan shook his head in reply. We sipped our teas.

"Hey Chandu, Why are you Sad?" Anvitha said plaintively.

"Nothing I'm perfectly all right but papa is alone at home. I need to go; I will see you guys soon."

Chandan stood up and went off without even waving us bye.

As soon as that Apoorva kept her half emptied cup back on table, stood up and shouted-"Chandan wait, even I've some work to do, I'll come with you."

She hugged Anvitha, waved me bye in hurry and followed Chandan. I gazed them for a while and cursed myself for my mistake.

"It's not only Chandan who likes Apoorva; I think even Apoorva likes Chandan." I told myself.

We denude our teas.

"Shall we move teddy?" Anvitha asked me.

"Wait here, I'll pay the bill and will be right back."

I said and went inside tea house near Shyam mama.

"What is special Roshan, today you seemed so happy?" Shyam mama asked me.

"Mama it was fun making Chandan a fool." I laughed.

"What are you saying Roshan?"

"Mama, do you know Chandu has started liking Apoorva without even telling us. So I've shocked him today saying that am already in love with her." I said laughing.

"Roshan, this is not funny, when will you learn being serious in life? You know how sensitive Chandan is right? Tell him the truth as soon as possible."

I stopped laughing and nodded, I paid the bill, waved bye to mama-"I will tell him tomorrow mama." I shouted and came out.

"Teddy, why did you take so long to pay the bill?" Anvitha back lashed.

I winked at her and held her hands, we walked back home.

¥ ¥ ¥

Anvitha opened her laptop and logged on to her profile. She was amazed when a message made its way into her inbox from Shravan Rao. She clicked on 'open message' button. The message read -"You look great in your dp Anvitha."

Anvitha noticed he was still online.

"Thank you sir" Anvitha replied him.

Within a couple of seconds there was a message from Shravan.

Shravan Rao: Eheheh…. Don't call me sir; treat me as your friend.

Anvitha Charan: Okay Shravan thank you ☺

Shravan Rao: So where was that picture taken?

Anvitha Charan: Why???

Shravan Rao: Because background looks beautiful too ☺

Anvitha Charan: It was taken in our Moonlight Streets.

Shravan Rao: MOONLIGHT STREETS!!! It sounds unique, where is it???

Anvitha Charan: In Ooty.

Shravan Rao: Right... So, how is your modeling career? I swear I was stunned looking at you on show!!!

Anvitha Charan: Thanks a lot Shravan☺ well, my career is still the same.

Shravan Rao: Do you like shooting ads???

Anvitha Charan: I may do if I get some good and decent offers ☺

Shravan Rao: Good...

Anvitha Charan: So where is your business based in???

Shravan Rao: At Palace city ☺ Mysore...

Anvitha Charan: Cool...

Shravan Rao: Not as cool as Ooty. :P

Anvitha Charan: Lol, Okay Shravan I got to go. Bye...

Shravan Rao: Ok Anvitha... Take care. ☺

Anvitha closed her laptop with a cute smile on her face. She felt good about Shravan and chuckled out.

¥ ¥ ¥

A postmaster stopped his cycle in front of Chandan's house and rang his noisy bell. Papa continued ironing clothes under the shed and looked at postman. Postman went up to papa.

"Who is Chandan Ram Prasad here?" postman asked papa.

"He is my son, not at home now" papa replied curious.

"Not a problem, here is a letter for him" Postman said and placed a letter in papa's hands.

Papa took it inside. Chandan reached home in the evening.

"Chandan come here" Papa called him.

"What papa" Chandan said and went near papa.

"There is a letter for you, check where it has come from" papa handed Chandan the letter.

Chandan received it, opened and started reading the letter.

"I've got job in Mysore papa" Chandan tilted up.

Papa felt extremely happy, He hugged Chandan and kissed him with excess of love. Chandan still had a sluggish face, but he faked his smile in reply to papa.

"When are you supposed to join???" Papa said delighted.

"Actually this letter has reached us a week later papa, now I have to join, within three days." Chandan said.

Chandan was sunk in the ocean of sadness.

"What are you thinking Chandan?" papa shook him.

"Papa I have to leave Ooty tonight"

Papa stared at the photo-frame of the God for a while, he gasped and nodded.

"Go for it Chandan, where ever you go be happy" Papa blessed him.

"Papa can you do me a favor?"

"What Chandan? Do you want more money?" Papa laughed.

"No, can you please iron my clothes for me today?"

"Sure Chandan" Papa said and took his clothes to iron.

Tears filled Chandan's eyes. He made his heart strong enough to leave Ooty because he longed for an environmental change; he rubbed his tears from his cheeks.

Chandan started packing his luggage, with his academic certificates, report cards and other stuffs. Meanwhile he started conversing within him.

"Should I inform my friends about my departure??? Am I doing it right or is it wrong??? Does Roshan really love Apoorva so much??? Is Apoorva someone's girl??? Am I a sinner for having crush on my best friend's girl??? After all it was just a crush; not even a love. Of course I'm a sinner, how can I show my face to Apoorva and Roshan? Yes, Roshan is the perfect match for her. Indeed am doing it right, I need to leave Ooty, I need to be refreshed."

Chandan hit his head for having crush on Apoorva; he hated everything that happened to him that day. He rubbed tears over and over.

"Its 10pm Chandan" Papa shouted from kitchen.

Chandan gulped, cleared his voice and shouted back-"No worries papa, bus is at 12am, if I take bath am ready."

After an hour, Chandan stood in front of papa, dressed in black shirt and pant.

"Did you inform this to your friends?" Papa asked.

"Not necessary papa" Chandan said in low voice.

"Are you doing it right?"

"I don't have sense about rights and wrong papa." Chandan said and bowed down to touch papa's feet.

"Be happy throughout your life Chandu" Papa said and brought him up. Chandan lifted his luggage and went out. Papa followed him.

"Okay Papa I'll move; take care of your health." Chandan said in crestfallen voice.

Papa nodded, tears filled his eyes. He tugged Chandan near and hugged him. Chandan stayed in his arms for a while and came out.

Chandan walked alone on the Moonlight streets, in that mid-night towards Ooty government bus stand. Papa gazed at him until he disappeared from his sight.

¥ ¥ ¥

Unknowingly my eyes grew wet. Oshini sunk completely in my story. Sun was just winding up for the day. Smooth rays of sun hit Oshini's cheek and she looked cuter. Train continued its speed. Oshini didn't agitate to console me. I wiped my tears without speaking a word.

"Chandan… Chandan was an innocent man" Oshini said staring at me in a hypnotized way.

I nodded bending my head in agony.

"Roshan, you should have not done this, not at least to Chandan, he is really a gentleman." Oshini said looking out from window and beamed.

"You don't seem like coming out of Chandan's world" I said smiling.

"I like Chandan for what he is." Oshini said focusing her look back at me. I smiled at her.

"Why did you lie to Chandan? When you didn't love Apoorva in real?" Oshini asked me and took a water bottle out of her bag.

"I agree that I didn't love her that day but later…" I dragged it and paused.

"Later…?" Oshini dragged it too, questioning me in a curious look.

¥ ¥ ¥

A night has passed. Next evening Anvitha called me.

"Hey Queen." I answered the call and said.

"Teddy, come to tea house, right now." Anvitha said in a resent voice.

"Is everything okay???"

"Come here now, I need to speak to you." Anvitha said and disconnected the call.

Anvitha never spoke this way before; I was at six and sevens. I got dressed up quickly and took out my phone to call Chandan near tea house, to tell him the truth but later I realized; that anyhow he will be present in tea house too and kept back my phone in pocket.

I rode to 4th cross, when I rode in front of corner mansion, I glanced the mansion's garden in search of Apoorva. Since I found none in the mansion, I sped up to Shyam mama's tea house. I parked my bike out and went under the bower. Apoorva was already there, Anvitha sat next to Apoorva resting her forehead on her palm. I didn't find Chandan, I sat next to Anvitha and pulled her hand, she dropped her head a bit down.

"Teddy when will you learn being serious in life?" Anvitha glared at me.

"Why are you so dull?" I said looking at Anvitha. On the other side Apoorva was dull too.

"Teddy, Chandan has left Ooty last night" Anvitha said woefully.

A feeling of tort occurred all over me when I heard it.

"Why?" I asked Anvitha with a complete dismay.

"He has got a job in Mysore." Anvitha answered me.

I was relieved after listening to it. I gasped, but still there was no end for the questions that my heart throwed on me but I stayed dumb at them.

"How did you know about his job?"

"Chandan had called me" Anvitha said and looked at Shyam mama, who brought us tea.

I looked up at Shyam mama, his face was sulked. He served us tea and went in. Apoorva pushed her cup back and looked aside. I went behind Shyam mama; we went into the tea house.

"What mama?" I asked.

"Finally you didn't tell Chandan the truth" Shyam mama said in a sad face.

"I don't understand why you are taking it so serious, he has got a good job and we all knew how badly he wanted a job. May be he was hurrying for it and that is why he had left Ooty without informing us." I said trying to convince Shyam mama.

"Who knows what feelings he had inside?" Shyam mama said and sneered.

I looked aside.

"At least now you should tell him the truth Roshan." Shyam mama advised me.

"What truth should I say him mama? It was just a crush, not even a love. Unnecessarily we are dragging this topic. I think we should stop it here." I said antagonized.

Shyam mama walked away without speaking a word. Blue hills swallowed the evening sun; moon was absent that evening like Chandan did. Our street name sounded stupid that night.

¥ ¥ ¥

Chandan boarded an auto next morning to K.D Street, Jayalakshmipuram from his hotel. He changed his connection to a new local sim.

Auto stopped in front of his office at K.D Street. Chandan got down and paid his auto fair. He walked into the office with his offer letter. Chandan occupied one of the seats in waiting hall. The H.R Manager came up to Chandan and took him into the managing director's cabin to introduce their new employee. Chandan went in and stood in front of young managing director. He noticed the name plate on the table and confirmed the director's name was "Shravan Rao."

The H.R manager introduced Chandan to Shravan Rao. They shook their hands, Shravan Rao asked Chandan to take his seat.

"Glad to meet you Chandan, we are happy to have an M.B.A topper as our assistant marketing manager here. I believe you work hard to do your bit, which adds to the company's success." Shravan said and smiled.

"I'll make sure that I keep up your hopes sir" Chandan said and nodded.

"And we also have accommodation and food facilities for you, feel free to use them."

"Sure sir, thank you for that."

"By the way where are you from?"

"Am from Ooty sir"

"Ooty!!! Oh, yeah nice place" Shravan said and chuckled out.

"Yes sir, it is." Chandan said in heavy heart.

"Well you may go now" Shravan said and focused back on his laptop.

Peon pulled the door towards him.

Chandan and the H.R. Manager walked out with the smiling face.

¥ ¥ ¥

"Hello, am I speaking to Ms. Apoorva Ramesh?" Dr. Parinitha said on phone.

"Yes speaking" Apoorva said looking at her hairs in the mirror.

"This is doctor Parinitha, from AISHC."

"Hello doctor, how are you?"

"Am fine Apoorva, thank you, by the way can you please come down to our hospital in the evening?"

"Sure but why doctor?"

"We need to speak to you; we will be waiting for you here. Bye."

"All right doctor, bye" Apoorva hanged phone in addled eyes.

Dr. Parinitha's call totally put Apoorva at sea; she slowly walked all around their living room thinking about the call. Finally Apoorva decided to visit AISHC with Anvitha. She dialed to Anvitha.

"Hi Apoorva how are you?" Anvitha said and looked at her laptop screen.

"Am fine, listen are you free today? We will go to AISHC. Dr. Parinitha had called me; it seems she needs to speak to me face to face."

Anvitha was silent for a while; she read Shravan's text and replied it.

"Anvitha, are you there?" Apoorva inquired.

"Oh... Yeah! But Apoorva am a bit busy, I have show's practice today." Anvitha lied and simultaneously replied a winking smiley for Shravan's text.

"Oh... No." Apoorva gasped.

"Go with Chandan."

"With Chandan???" Apoorva questioned Anvitha's unexpected reply.

"Oh... Sorry, I forgot the fact that he is out of Ooty. Ok you do this, you go with Roshan, and I'll ask him to pick you" Anvitha said and chuckled out seeing Shravan's reply.

"With Roshan???" Apoorva asked in hesitant voice.

"Yeah... he is free today. I'll call him and will tell him to be near your home. You be ready. Bye" Anvitha said and disconnected the call.

Apoorva brought down her phone from ear with a positive feel.

"Is it good to go with Roshan?" Apoorva conversed herself, "Why not, I thought Chandan was a really good friend of mine but as he said, he had no one to spend time around and hence he spent his time with me. I was just a time pass friend for him; otherwise he would have informed me about his departure from Ooty. He lost his place in my mind. Yes I will go with Roshan." Apoorva came out of all these and entered her room to get dressed.

¥ ¥ ¥

Anvitha called me and forced me to go out for AISHC with Apoorva, I agreed and hung up. After I got dressed, I got a message, I opened it.

"What time are you coming at; I'm waiting here."

It was an unknown number, later I understood that, it was Apoorva. I didn't reply her back, I rode towards 4th cross. I stopped my bike in front of mansion. Apoorva stood waiting for me near gate. She was gorgeously dressed in yellow plain langha dhavani with accessories that were meant to match the attire. Her smile was filled with serenity that made everything around her look beautiful as well. I was completely taken aback and immaterialized everything material for few brief moments. She walked up to me.

"Shall we move?" I said getting back to senses.

"Okay" She said and smiled.

I started my bike. Apoorva's face said her hesitation to sit behind me in the same bike.

"No issues get on" I said.

She placed her right hand on my shoulder. I felt an electrifying sensation which enlightened everything around me. Moonlight Street looked just exquisite and she was the absolute reason for it.

When I rode in front of tea house, Shyam mama looked at us in dropped jaws. He was consternated to see us on same bike.

"Do you know AISHC?" Apoorva asked in a cushy tone.

"I've heard about it, but I don't know the way to it."

"Okay, then I'll direct you the way." Apoorva said and pointed her finger towards the right ways.

We rode without speaking anything interesting. After about an hour of riding, we reached AISHC. I parked my bike; Apoorva got down and told me to follow her. When I entered the building, I was dismayed to see dumb and deaf children playing in one corner of the hall and I also noticed blind children in the other hall.

Apoorva wished a lady doctor and spoke to her for a while. The lady took Apoorva into Doctor's chamber; Apoorva turned to me and called me in. I followed her into the cabin. Apoorva introduced me to the Dean and we shook our hands.

Apoorva hugged a small girl, who sat on the chair blind folded. Dean untied the medical tape from the girl's eyes and asked her to open her eyes slowly. The girl scrunched her eyes thrice and finally opened it clearly. The girl was excited and shouted that she could see things around. Apoorva was up in the sky of Euphoria, she kissed the girl, and the girl hugged Apoorva and shouted -"Thank you akka."

I gasped, walked out of the chamber and reached the main door of AISHC. I noticed a small dumb boy, who struggled to catch a colorful butterfly, which sat on one of the flowers in the garden. Each time when he tried catching it, the butterfly flew away. I went to him and signaled him not to make sound; the boy placed his finger on lips and nodded. I acted dumb with him. I slowly crawled towards the butterfly and at one stroke I held its wings, the boy jumped happily clapping. I passed the butterfly to his hands; he held it and inspected it from all the angles. I had no words to expound that innocent joys, I cherished the moment. The boy hugged me happily and placed a kiss on my forehead. I kissed him back and turned behind.

Apoorva stood at the main door in folded arms, and watched all these. I smiled scratching head. For the first time Apoorva gave me a real smile wholeheartedly. I chuckled out.

"Shall we move?" Apoorva said and smiled again.

I nodded and we walked out towards my bike. The boy clapped his hands, we turned back to look at him, he stretched his lips and waved us bye, we waved him back.

I kick started my bike, this time Apoorva got on my bike in a blissful face.

"Apoorva…" I called out her name loudly for the 1st time.

"Tell me Roshan." Apoorva said in a bland voice.

"You have done a good job."

"I wish doing more Roshan, but am financially helpless."

"Never mind but still this is great Apoorva."

"That was just a financial support Roshan, but the real joy is what you gave to that dumb boy today, that is exorbitant."

"I like you Apoorva."

"Like???" Apoorva grinned.

"Yes, I mean the way you live for others."

"In that case I like you loads Roshan."

"It's not that way Apoorva, I did it because I know the pain of orphans."

She nodded, we continued our poignant conversation. Darkness covered all around us, sun was set to sleep in west. We reached Moonlight streets as late as 8:30pm.

I stopped my bike in front of the mansion. Apoorva got down and called me in. I declined saying it was too late. She looked at my face closely and thanked me. I smiled in return. Her tiny eyes took my heart away.

"Good night Roshan" She wished me.

I wished her back and started my bike. She walked inside the mansion. I rode to my home. I realized Apoorva was a gentle person but not an arrogant girl. Though I liked her, I still believed, she well pairs only my best friend Chandan.

"Yes, Chandan is the suitable man for her." I said to myself and walked into home.

¥ ¥ ¥

Anvitha came back home from modeling school; She rushed to her room and logged on to her profile.

"Hey Shravan" She pinged Shravan Rao.

Anvitha waited for five more minutes and texted him again; after about half an hour, there was a message from Shravan.

Shravan Rao: "Hello gorgeous."

Anvitha Charan:" Don't speak to me. ☹"

Shravan Rao: "Sorry dear… I was held up with meeting."

Anvitha Charan: "I said, am not speaking to you."

Shravan Rao: "1000 sorrys…"

Anvitha Charan: "Okay excused."

Shravan Rao: "Thank you sweet heart."

Anvitha Charan: "Sweet heart =-o?"

Shravan Rao: "Just like that."

Anvitha Charan: "Shravan I've got an ad offer from 'glinting clothes' company. Do you think I should accept it?"

Shravan Rao: "Anvitha… have you thought twice about it?"

Anvitha Charan: "I don't really know much about the company. Which is why, am asking your suggestion."

Shravan Rao: "Well, if you ask me, you shouldn't accept it dear. Don't you know their scam?"

After about twenty minutes.

Shravan Rao: Are you there?

Anvitha Charan:" Shravan… there is some problem with my id, am unable to send message in time, just call me whenever you are free, I will be waiting for your call, bye ☺ Take care dear."

Anvitha left her phone number to Shravan and logged off. She closed her laptop and looked at her face in mirror, her cheeks turned red and she smiled to herself.

Shravan was exhilarated to see Anvitha's phone number on screen and he chuckled out. Peon gave Shravan a dirty look.

That night Anvitha got a call from an unknown number. She picked up the line. Anvitha heard a strange manly "Hello."

Anvitha 'Helloed' back.

There was a lightening all over Shravan's system; he was thrilled listening to her melody. Shravan didn't speak a word until Anvitha brought him back from her second hello.

"Hi Anvitha, Shravan here" He said.

"I got to know it was you Shravan."

"How did you know?"

"My mind told me." Anvitha said blushing and came out on terrace.

"Your mind? Cool… what did your heart say then?" Shravan bantered.

"Excuse me boss, come back on ground." Anvitha said and giggled.

"Of course am flying, your mind is sooo dear to me to predict my call" Shravan said proudly.

"It was an inter-state number dear that is how I knew it was you."

"Oh… Damn" Shravan bit his tongue.

Anvitha laughed and continued-"So shouldn't I accept that offer?"

"According to me, no you should not consider it da."

"Okay…" Anvitha said in sad tone.

"No worries Anvitha, you'll get a better one soon." Shravan persuaded her.

"Thank you Shravan"

"Anything for you dear" Shravan said and smiled.

"Why is it so?" Anvitha asked in suspicious.

"Because, I like you" Shravan blurted.

"You like me?" Anvitha repeated expecting an explanation for his statement.

"Yeah… generally… I mean, yes I like you as a good person, I mean like, like a good friend." Shravan stuttered.

Anvitha laughed out loud.

They continued their conversation with laugh and jokes.

¥ ¥ ¥

I came downstairs yawing and rubbing my eyes. Jasmine was watching television and ate breakfast on sofa. I sat next to her and rested my head on her shoulder, feeling sleepy yet.

"Roshan, is it a time to wake up?" Jasmine said and caressed my hairs…

"What work do I have Jasmine?"

"Whatever, a healthy person always wakes up before sun."

"Okay darling, I'll wake up soon from tomorrow" I said and looked up at her.

Jasmine laughed and asked whether I want tea. I nodded; Jasmine stood up and went into the kitchen. I laid on sofa and changed channels.

"You will drink tea only if you brush your teeth."-Jasmine shouted from kitchen, while adding tea dust to boiling water.

I crunched my face, walked up to washbowl and brushed my teeth. After a while Jasmine brought tea and passed it to me saying-"Good boy."

I smiled while receiving tea. She sat next to me watching television again. I sipped tea.

"So how is Chandan at Mysore?" Jasmine asked concentrating on television.

I looked at her face which was watching television interestingly. I didn't know what to reply.

"He is doing well." I lied her, though I didn't had his contact.

"So to look after Ram Prasad is yours and Anvitha's duty now."

"We will Jasmine." I said and nodded.

"Good… when are you going to take a job like him Roshan?" Jasmine said and looked at me.

"Very soon Jasmine"

"And when is your C.S results supposed to be out?"

"Shortly Jasmine, may be within a couple of weeks." I said and placed empty cup on table.

Jasmine pushed me to get freshen up. I walked into the shower in no heart.

¥ ¥ ¥

Shravan and Anvitha's relationship got firm proceedings. They are very close to each other now and spend half of their day speaking to each others on phone. Though Shravan was busy in his business, he always had time to catch up Anvitha on phone. That evening Shravan called up Anvitha. Anvitha picked up and wished him.

"There's a good news, guess what?" Shravan shouted.

"What is that?" Anvitha was curious.

"Am coming to Ooty next month on business, somehow I'll make time to catch you up."

"Are you sure Shravan? I'm excited man." Anvitha shouted back.

"Yes Anvitha, finally we are meeting… this is the time, I waited for from six months."

"Same here Shravan, I'm waiting to see you." Anvitha said in blossomed eyes.

"Lovely dear… Okay I'll call you back in minutes."

"Wait Shravan, I think we need to speak a lot, when we meet. Make extra time for that." Anvitha said and smiled.

"Sure dear, I think we really need to speak a lot." Shravan said gulping; his heart uplifted its beats.

"Okay, call me back when you go free." Anvitha said and hung up.

Anvitha throwed her phone on bed, ran to calendar and counted the days left to see Shravan in Moonlight streets.

¥ ¥ ¥

It had been three months since Chandan shifted to his office's accommodation. That day Chandan completed his personal work and reached office two hours late. Chandan entered his cabin and picked up some files. Peon came in and asked Chandan to meet managing director. Chandan was perplexed. He stood up and walked into Shravan Rao's cabin.

"Good morning sir" Chandan wished and smiled at Shravan.

Shravan looked up at Chandan's face – "Half an hour more to call it a good afternoon Chandan" Shravan said showing his watch at Chandan.

"Am sorry for being late sir" Chandan looked down.

"I can understand if it had been a day's problem Chandan, but you are doing this continuously from twenty days. I appreciate your marvelous work for our company. I know from last two months how much of profit our company has earned because of you. If you have any personal problems, please let us know Chandan. If we can help you out, we will surely do it for you." Shravan Rao said politely.

"Am again sorry for being late continuously sir, I promise it won't affect my responsibilities here and I look on not to repeat it again." Chandan said in sunken voice.

"Chandan am saying it again, if you have any problems even here; let us know to fix it."

"No, I have absolutely got a good working place sir. If I need any help from your end for my personal problem, I'll really ask you. Thank you for being nice with me sir, it instigates me to work hard for our company." Chandan said and smiled.

Shravan's phone vibrates to Anvitha's call.

"That is okay, I believe you won't do this henceforth. We don't want to lose you Chandan. You can go now." Shravan said and took up the call.

Chandan walked out in stressed out face.

¥ ¥ ¥

I had been to outskirts of Ooty to fix some bank issues of Jasmine. After completing bank's work and when I was way back home, I passed by AISHC. I recalled the girl and dumb boy; soon I went to the nearby sweets store and walked into AISHC, with two bags full of sweets.

As soon as I walked in, the same dumb boy came running and hugged me. I went down and kissed his cheeks. I passed one bag of sweets that I bought for them. The dumb boy was happy seeing me and sweets. I walked inside the other hall, where blind children played. I found the girl who got her eyes by Apoorva's donation. I went to her and started speaking to her; I gave the other bag of sweets to the blind children. The sight of those children panicked me. I started playing with them. They were all delighted.

Dr.Parinitha came up and wished me; I turned and wished her back. I spoke with Parinitha for one more hour about their hospital and dumb children. When night arrived, I wished her bye and left AISHC.

As soon as I left AISHC, Dr.Parinitha called up Apoorva.

"Hello doctor, how are you?" Apoorva received the call and said.

"Am fine Apoorva, thank you and how are you doing?" Dr.Parinitha inquired.

"I'm good as well doctor." Apoorva said and smiled.

"Why you didn't turn up to our centre with Roshan today?"

"With Roshan? What are you saying doctor?" Apoorva was startled.

"Yes, he had been to our centre today, he is such a genuine person Apoorva. He brought sweets to our children and played with them. No one visits us regularly like this and make our children happy, all our children ask for him."

"Oh… is it, well, Roshan didn't inform me about his visiting to AISHC doctor. We will visit you again soon."

"Okay Apoorva keep visiting us, bye."

"Bye doctor" Apoorva hung up.

She walks out to balcony.

"Roshan is not just a person, he have got a great personality in him. He is not an arrogant guy. He is genuine, lovable and winsome man." Apoorva said to herself. She blushed out.

¥ ¥ ¥

Anvitha woke up early than usual that day. That was the day, Shravan was supposed to meet Anvitha in Moonlight streets. Anvitha imagined Shravan's face in her mind; she recalled everything that she had planned to speak with him. She was excited and waited to see Shravan.

On the other side, she kept this as a secret with all of us, to give us a surprise. Anvitha opened her closet to choose good attire. She took most of them out. After an hour, finally she selected an outfit for that evening. Anvitha took out her phone and dialed Shravan. Shravan picked up the line after a while.

"Helloooo…" Anvitha shouted in excitement.

"Hi…" Shravan said.

"Where are you now?"

"I just passed by Nanjangud, it takes three more hours to reach Ooty."

"Three more hours? Well, I expected you here by now."

Shravan spoke out before Anvitha could complete.-"Hey listen, what place should I reach to, in Ooty?"

"When you reach Ooty, ask someone for Moonlight lamp spot, it's quite a famous spot here and anyone can show you the way."

"Okay." Shravan said.

"Anvithaaa..." Pushpa aunty shouted.

"Coming Amma" Anvitha shouted back covering the speaker of phone.

Shravan smiled and waited for her bye, since he knew her next word.

"Okay Shravan call me when you are here. Waiting to see you, bye"

"Sure, bye take care da." Shravan said and hung up.

¥ ¥ ¥

I got 2nd class in C.S exam. Jasmine was more than relieved to know that I at least managed to crack the exams. Jasmine planned a nice lunch for that day and informed me to call my friends for lunch including Apoorva.

I didn't want to list Apoorva as my friend, since she had already crossed the border of being just friend in my mind, I still forcefully tried forgetting it, believing Apoorva was meant for Chandan and not to cheat my best friend on Apoorva.

On the other hand, I felt bad for not being able to convey my results to Chandan. I never missed sharing either my happiness or my sorrows with him any day. I dialed to his number but as usually it said that the customer had stopped using their service.

Jasmine smiled at me and walked into the kitchen to prepare lunch. I informed Jasmine that I would visit tea house and I came out of home. I called Anvitha many times; she picked it up at my 6th attempt.

"Sorry teddy, I was a bit busy, that is why I couldn't take your call." Anvitha said pleasing me.

"That's ok Queen, there is good news for you." I said.

"Same here Teddy, meet me in tea house at evening, there is a surprise for you."

"Fine and can you make up for lunch at my home today?"

"Oh...Teddy bear, sorry... am a bit busy. Anyhow we will meet in tea house right?"

"Sure Queen, ok carry on, bye, take care." I said and hung up.

I thought of going to tea house but I remembered Apoorva. Since I never visited her home any day, inviting her over phone didn't seemed good to me.

I walked up to the mansion. I knocked mansion's main door. Radha aunty opened the door.

"Hi Roshan… Come in." Aunty said seeing me.

I gave her a smile and entered in. I looked all around a huge living hall to find Apoorva.

"How is Jasmine doing?" Radha aunty said passing me tea.

"She is fine aunty and I have come to see Apoorva." I said and received the tea cup.

"Apoorva… see who has come." Aunty shouted in Kannada, rearranging the flower that she wore.

"Coming Amma" Apoorva shouted back from upstairs.

I sipped tea and stared the staircase often, expecting her arrival. Apoorva came down, drying her wet hair from a towel. She looked outstandingly gorgeous in her dropping wet hairs.

"Hi Roshan…" Apoorva said continuing while drying her hairs.

I wished her back.

"I thought of calling you, nice that at least today you made time to visit my home."

"Why? Do you want to take me to the AISHC again?" I banter Apoorva.

"No because you alone went to AISHC with sweets to children yesterday." Apoorva said and gave me a deep divine look.

I wasn't able to figure out, what that look meant.

"Well, there is a surprise for you." I said.

"Surprise? What is that?" Apoorva said and gave me a curious smile.

"I will let you know later; by the way I came here to invite you for a lunch at my home. Please do come."

"What is special Roshan?"

"I said I'll tell you later right" I said and stood up.

I announced my departure. Apoorva came up to door, I smiled at her and walked back home.

¥ ¥ ¥

Exactly at 3pm, there was a calling bell in our home. Jasmine opened the door. Apoorva stood in a smiling face. Apoorva hugged Jasmine and wished her. Jasmine was happy seeing Apoorva.

I turned television off and wished Apoorva. Apoorva wished me back in a smiling face. Jasmine called us for lunch, we went to the table. Three of us ate lunch with some interesting conversation.

Jasmine was impressed by Apoorva's behavior.

"Wow… nice sketch, who did it?" Apoorva asked looking at Jasmine's sketch framed on wall.

"I sketched it." I said.

"Roshan, do you sketch?" Apoorva exclaimed.

I nodded.

"Will you show me your collection?"

"By all means" I said.

I went up to my cupboard and brought her some of my sketches. Apoorva took it with amazement and eager. She opened the first sketch.

"Hey this looks like you, Anvitha and Chandan in your childhood." Apoorva said in saucer eyes.

"Yes and this is Mother Mercy Paul" I said turning to next sketch.

"Oh… Yeah Chandan had told me about her once." Apoorva said recalling.

"All sketches are extraordinary but why in all of these sketches lip portion is incomplete?" Apoorva asked closing all sketches.

"I don't know drawing the lip portion Apoorva." I said and hung my face. She lifted my head up.

"So you didn't like these sketch right?" I asked in a sunken face.

"No, I just love them; they are all fabulous but try being complete in all aspects of life Roshan, it can be either a sketch or being in love. Just be a complete man" Apoorva said in a shy face, she indirectly instigated me to propose her.

Apoorva got call from Queen. She called me and Apoorva to tea house. We informed Jasmine about Queen's call and left home. Jasmine came up to door and waved us bye.

I crushed my body with my arms to avoid cold. Apoorva walked close to me. Every step with her felt magical. Day on day our relationship started perplexing me. I was surprised to see an Audi car in front of tea house, we walked in. The same person who asked me the way to Moonlight lamp spot in the afternoon, stood a bit close to Anvitha. Anvitha looked at us. She introduced that man as Shravan Rao to me.

"He is the one who showed me the way to lamp spot Anvitha." Shravan said shaking hands with me.

Anvitha then introduced Apoorva to him. Before Shravan could extend his hand to shake, Apoorva wished him in her folded palms, like she did with me. Shravan wished her back the same way laughing.

I was Euphoric, seeing it. I understood Apoorva didn't mean to humiliate me that day but she had never forgotten her roots. That particular misunderstanding I had on her got cleared, that moment. I gave Apoorva the happiest smile ever. She raised her eyebrow questioning my happiness. Anvitha observed all our actions and smiled the way she discovered some secret. We all sat on our chairs, Shyam mama arrived to take orders, and we ordered four teas. Anvitha said Shravan about our friendship from our childhood. Shyam mama returned with teas and passed us. He gave Shravan a strange look and saw me.

"He is Shravan Rao Anvitha's" I paused for a while and said "Friend."

Anvitha and Shravan exchanged their looks.

"Finally there is someone to replace someone else's place in Moonlight streets." Shyam mama said in a killing smile.

Shravan asked Anvitha what Shyam mama meant. Anvitha smiled and asked him to ignore it.

"Teddy my surprise is out, now tell me about yours." Anvitha asked sipping tea.

Every one focused their looks on me.

"I have passed C.S exams and I have interview next week, I may leave Ooty soon." I said looking at Apoorva.

"Are you going out of Moonlight streets?" Apoorva asked me in a worried tone.

I nodded.

"Moonlight streets sound so unique, how did these streets earn that name?" Shravan asked changing the topic to lighten the atmosphere.

Anvitha and I looked each other faces blinking without knowing an answer for his question.

Shyam mama chuckled out, came closer and said-"I will tell you. Have you all seen Moonlight lamp in front of our streets?"

We all gave him a nod.

"Yes, that is 200 years old lamp. When the collector of Coimbatore, John Sullivan visited Ooty for the first time in 1819, he was enthralled by the beauty of this place. In the same year, Sullivan began the construction of the first European dwelling on these hills. Ooty served as the summer capital of madras presidency. In 1830 Sullivan realized the need for a street light, which could light up the whole small village of Ooty and hence he started the construction of a huge lamp. The construction was completed in 1831 and this lamp was called India's longest lamp of that time. Since the light of this lamp resembled exactly the original Moonlight, all villagers started calling it the Moonlight lamp. Being 200 years old lamp, it still works very well."

"200 years old lamp, still works good!" Shravan said in his wondering eyes.

"Quiet." Anvitha said turning to Shravan and focused back on Shyam mama.

"As the town got developed, new streets were constructed in front of this lamp and to co-incident it, these four streets end exactly where this lamp's spreading light ends at, which is why people called it the Moonlight streets." Shyam mama said and gulped.

His story reminded me of school days history class. I gasped out. Shyam mama took back all denude cups.

"Anvitha its time for me, Shall we move?" Shravan looked at his watch and whispered in Anvitha's ear.

"Bye Teddy, Shravan is leaving, I'll meet you tomorrow, bye Apoorva." Anvitha said and stood up.

Shravan shook my hand. They waved bye to Shyam mama and got into car.

"Shall we move?" I said looking at Apoorva.

She kept quiet like she didn't hear anything. I shook Apoorva and repeated it again.

"Roshan, do you necessarily have to go out of Ooty?" Apoorva asked in dull tone.

"Why are you asking this?"

"Anvitha is very busy in her life like you know. I can't imagine how I will manage all alone here, if you go out it makes me lonely." Apoorva said maintaining a neutral expression in her face.

I was touched when Apoorva said it. I looked at her without speaking.

"Anyhow all the best" She said pulling my hand to give a handshake.

Her eyes filled with tears, which she tried hiding from me and walked away not waiting for me. I stayed there, thinking about Apoorva and that different way she behaved with me that day. I felt like I was special in her life.

¥ ¥ ¥

I went in tea house. Apoorva sat on a chair, waiting for me.

"Where is Queen?" I asked Apoorva taking my seat.

"She has not yet come."

"She said she would be here by now." I said looking at my watch.

Apoorva shrugged. I opened my phone to text Anvitha.

"So how was your interview last week?" Apoorva asked me giving a firm look.

"Nothing great to discuss" I said and looked aside.

Meanwhile I got a text from Anvitha which said she will meet me in the evening.

"What are you saying?" Apoorva was puzzled.

"I didn't attend it." I said keeping back my phone in pocket.

"Why Roshan?" Apoorva's eyes were concerned.

"Because I don't want to make you alone here" I said looking into her eyes.

Her eyes blossomed, but she managed to hide it from me.

"Got the reason?" I said.

Apoorva looked down, bit her lip and smiled. It was difficult to withdraw my gaze from her. We didn't speak for about ten minutes. She brushed back her hairs away from her eyes. Our eyes met though we were silent, our eyes started communicating.

Without any clue, my false statement with Chandan on Apoorva was turning true. I got back to senses. I broke our eye contact and looked aside.

"Thank you for your concern on me Roshan." She said and blushed.

Apoorva didn't wait for my reply, she got on her vehicle and left. I fixed my look at her, until she disappeared from my sight.

"Before this relationship gets serious, I better wipe off this intangible affection and focus on patching up Apoorva with Chandan. They are made for each others. They are of same velocity. I can never deceive my best friend." I told myself. But it was difficult to get over her.

¥ ¥ ¥

Next evening I got Anvitha's call. She said me to meet her. I got dressed and walked out. Anvitha waited for me in her garden.

"Good evening Queen." I wished Anvitha.

"Hi Teddy, how are you?" Anvitha wished me back hugging.

Anvitha looked the hottest that day. She was dressed in off shoulder dress.

"Am fine Queen, what kept you busy yesterday?" I asked Anvitha.

"As usually I have another show next week Teddy." We walked out of the compound.

"Great, so where are we going now?"

"1st cross to see papa, It had been ages since we visited him. It's our duty being Chandan's best friends to look after papa, when he is not here." Anvitha said and looked at me.

I gave her a nod,

We walked into papa's house. Papa was busy folding clothes. As soon as he saw us, he called us in. we sat beside him on the floor and spoke to him. After about half an hour, papa stood up to bring us tea. Anvitha cut him off and she went into the kitchen to prepare us tea. Papa brought a letter, that he received in the morning to me and asked me to read it for him. I opened the letter and started reading it.

"How are you papa? As of your wish finally am well settled in Mysore, I've a good job and am earning really well. I don't think I will let you continue the laundry business anymore. Within other couple of months, I'll take you with me, here. Am terribly missing you and Moonlight streets, and convey my big hi to Shyam mama. Bye papa, take care of your health."

I read it to papa and kept it aside. I was irked by Chandan's letter. I didn't find a word about me in it. I didn't understand why Chandan didn't think of me and Anvitha when he wrote it.

Anvitha brought us tea. Papa was happy with the letter. Anvitha observed a desperate change in my facial expression. She took her cup and sat beside me, inquiring about papa's health. After about an hour, we informed our departure to papa and stood up. Papa came up to the door and waved us bye.

"What happened Teddy?" Anvitha asked me, holding my shoulder, while we were walking back.

"Just leave it… Queen" I said.

"Tell me." Anvitha compelled me.

I told her about the letter. Anvitha was equally upset with it. We walked home in silence.

¥ ¥ ¥

Chandan's letter had been giving me a persistent prick although it had been a week since I read it. I never wanted to lose Chandan for anybody in the world. I didn't eat well for a week, his letter made a strong impact in my mind.

I went to tea house to forget it, Shyam mama brought me tea. I was not interested in anything. I held tea cup but lost my strength and dropped it down not being able to sip, cup broke down and made an annoying clatter, to which Shyam mama came. He asked what has happened to me. I didn't utter a word.

The day was just dawning and Moonlight streets lighted up. I came away from tea house and walked out of Moonlight streets since I was not interested to get back home. I was frustrated; I found a liquor shop by the way. I went in and bought a whiskey. Ooty was frozen to ice that night. I reached a lonely tea estate, I was all alone there. I opened the bottle and started boozing. Tear rolled down my eyes. I remembered Chandan over and over and the time spent with Apoorva. I was in a valley of sorrows. That was the first time ever I tasted liquor.

I received a call from Anvitha-"Hey Teddy!!!"

I was completely broken and high, that I couldn't comprehend her sweet polite voice.

"I've lost him Queen." I said, "I've lost my best friend. I've lost him completely. I've lost the one for whom I was supposed to be available. I'm not even in his mind when he needs someone." I was losing clarity in speech and didn't realize when I dropped my phone down.

When I woke up in the morning, Anvitha stood in front of me holding a tablet and a cup of tea in a tray. I rose from bed quickly and looked around to check where I was.

"You are in my home." Anvitha said passing me tea.

I received it and peeped out at hall.

"Don't worry; Amma and Appa are not here since two days, they have gone to visit our distinct relatives." Anvitha said looking into my eyes.

I sipped tea and hung my head down.

"Head ache?" Anvitha asked me lifting my head up from her hand.

I nodded. Anvitha passed me the tablet. I took tablet and looked out from the window.

"I don't like seeing you this way again." Anvitha glared at me.

I looked back at her.

"I can't see you like this Teddy." Her tone was softer this time.

I didn't speak to her. My eyes were shutting though I tried opening them forcefully.

I only remember Anvitha saying – "Sleep for some more time and take rest."

I dropped my head back on pillow.

¥ ¥ ¥

When I woke up, I looked at the clock and told myself its 5:30 in the evening.

"Oh…Damn I slept a lot." I said to myself and got out of bed.

I looked out of window; rain had just stopped after a heavy downpour. I felt fresh and light. My mind was calm and stress free. I walked out of the room and went into Anvitha's room in search of her. Anvitha was on her laptop.

"Hi Teddy, how are you feeling now?" she asked looking at me.

"Am feeling very light now, Queen." I said hardly smiling at her. I sat next to her.

"You haven't eaten anything since morning, just sit here, I'll bring you something." Anvitha said and walked out to kitchen.

She left her laptop opened beside me. I walked to washbowl and washed my face. I heard a beep sound from Anvitha's laptop. I went near it and saw a message from Shravan Rao, on screen. The message read- "I love you a lot honey." I rubbed my eyes and re-read it. I read it right, it was the same. Anvitha brought me a cup of tea and fried rice. I took it and started sipping tea. Anvitha went back to her laptop and continued her chat.

"What are you doing Queen?"

"Chatting with Shravan" Anvitha said still reading his message.

"What's going on between you?" I asked looking at her.

Anvitha raised her head and looked at me.

"Sorry Teddy, I should have told you this long back but I waited for right time to tell you this." She said and gulped-"We are in love Teddy."

"Love? Did you just say me its love?" I asked her in perplexed voice.

"Yes why?" Anvitha found it curious.

"Is it love or is it a crush?"

"Idiot" Anvitha laughed- "Crush is just an infatuation or an attraction to put it. Crushes happen like passing cloud. It can happen on one's attitude, appearance anything. You get crush for a mental picture for someone. It can't be true love. But true love kindles the feeling that your search for the life has ended." She said turned to her laptop, she saw Shravan's picture there and blushed.

"Are you sure?" I asked fully activated.

"Sure about what?" Anvitha asked giving me a weird look.

"That crush can't be love but simply an infatuation."

"Of course, am damn sure." Anvitha said and smiled.

I felt completely relieved all of a sudden. My muddled up feelings on Chandan and Apoorva vanished like a mist and my mind was devoted of guilt of being a cheater.

"Apoorva is mine forever and she is not suitable for anyone else. Physics says like poles always repel each others. Chandu and Apoorva may be of same wavelength and they may get along sooner than others but true love between them is impossible, but when I am with Apoorva I always feel my search for life has ended" I said myself and chuckled out.

"Teddy finish from your plate first" Anvitha said pointing at fried rice.

I pulled her front cut hair and laughed.

"Ouch… stupid!" Anvitha cheered and smiled herself, thinking I felt better.

¥ ¥ ¥

The following week, I got a call from Apoorva. She asked me to meet her in tea house. A week without seeing her felt like a year without rain. I was delighted to meet Apoorva. I was dressed to my best and I went to tea house. Apoorva was already there, she held Moonlights mails newspaper in her hand. I was quite lucky to see two moons at once that evening.

"One belongs to the sky and the other belongs to me." I said myself seeing Apoorva.

I went and stood behind her. I held her shoulder, Apoorva looked up suddenly but after knowing it was me, she blushed. I wished her she wished me back. I sat next to her. Apoorva opened newspaper again. Shyam mama bought us tea. We smiled at him, he returned us a formal smile and left.

"Roshan I have found an opening for assistant legal advisor job in a reputed Ooty company. You should try this." Apoorva said pointing to an ad in newspaper.

I stared at Apoorva. I felt Apoorva was concerned about me, I felt I was precious in her life, our relationship was exceptional. I didn't know why I felt that way specifically that day. I felt I was genuinely in love with her and realized am not cheating anyone on Apoorva.

"Roshan" Apoorva shook me.

"Oh… Yes." I said coming out of my deep thoughts.

"Will you attend this interview for me?" Apoorva asked holding my hands on table.

I felt the warmth of pure love.

"Certainly I will do Apoorva." I said holding back her hand trying to return her the same warmth.

"Roshan, if you get this job you can look after Jasmine well, above all you will get everything in life like money, fame, assets." Apoorva said caressing my hand.

"Those are not important in my life." I said losing myself in her eyes.

"Then what is important for you?" Apoorva asked still looking in my eyes.

"A girl who loves me truly, a girl for my life"

"How should your girl be like?"

"My girl should be very simple, like you" I said, It was a roundabout proposal for Apoorva.

Apoorva understood it.

"You have already got her. The only thing is you should discover her." Apoorva said, while she was keen to accept my proposal.

"Do you know why all men want girlfriend?" I asked her.

"Because behind every successful man there is a woman" Apoorva said and laughed.

"Oh… in that case I'll definitely hit success."

"How?" Apoorva asked perplexed.

"Because I just discovered my girl" I chaffed Apoorva.

Apoorva blushed. She took back her hand from my hold noticing Shyam mama's arrival.

"So when is my interview?" I faked a formal talk.

"I will let you know after inquiring the dates Roshan." Apoorva said.

Shyam mama took our denude cups and left.

"You're looking handsome Roshan." Apoorva said. Her cheeks turned red.

I bit my lower lip staring Apoorva.

¥ ¥ ¥

I looked at Jasmine, while she was adding sugar to tea. Her hands trembled.

"Jasmine is getting aged. I should get a job soon to look after her well." I said myself and kept gazing her.

Jasmine poured hot tea to two cups and handed me a cup. Jasmine took her cup and sat across the table.

"When will you get a job Roshan? Am not young anymore to look after you, I wish, I see you well settled and secured in life before I pass away." Jasmine said and a tear drop rolled down from her eye.

"Jasmine…" I said cutting her off and I held her mouth from my palm, not letting her to continue.

She removed my palm from her mouth and said- "Yes Roshan, you don't know how badly I wanted to see you going for a job like others."

"Don't worry Jasmine, I'll get a job soon and I will look after you well." I said and wiped her tears.

I stood up and sat next to her. There was a call on our landline. I walked up to it and received the call.

"Hello… Teddy" Anvitha sounded excited.

"Hello… Queen, what's happening?"

"Teddy… Guess what?" Anvitha was euphoric when she said it.

"Tell me what?" I found it curious.

"My parents are okay with Shravan and his family is coming to see me this Sunday, you and Apoorva should be with me the whole day." Anvitha rattled.

"Okay okay… we will be with you for sure." I promised her.

"Okay, Teddy bye, take care" Anvitha said and hung up.

I went back to Jasmine.

"So finally Anvitha is settled in life." Jasmine said and smiled.

I gave her a nod with a smile.

"Who is that guy?"

"Shravan Rao, an industrialist at Mysore. Seems like a good guy, had met him once." I said and turned to Jasmine.

Jasmine lit up candles in front of Jesus sculpture and prayed for Anvitha.

I leaned against wall smiling.

¥ ¥ ¥

Anvitha spent about three hours with mirror that day. For the very first time she wore salwar and looked extremely hot with a blushing face. Anvitha repeatedly asked how she looked to Pushpa aunty. When I reached Anvitha's home, Anvitha's father shook my hand and hosted me. He placed his hand around my shoulder and we walked in.

"Roshan, you've completed your education right?"

"Yes uncle." I said in a soft tone.

"Fine then get a job soon, Jasmine is struggling to see you being secured in life. She will be relieved, if you get a job." Uncle said patting my back.

"Will get one soon uncle." I said casually.

"Do you know how much she has sacrificed for you?" uncle said looking at me.

"What do you mean uncle?" I was confused.

"I think you don't know about her past, try knowing it at least now." he said and gestured me to get in.

I thought about it for a while and walked in. Pushpa aunty noticed me and brought me breakfast. Anvitha bumped and hugged me from behind.

"Hey Queen... you're looking gorgeous girl." I said in saucer eyes.

"Aww... Thank you Teddy." Anvitha said pulling my cheek.

I felt totally happy to see her euphoric and excited that day.

"Apoorva will never keep up her time. She said she will be here by now Teddy." Anvitha said crunching her face.

My blood rushed into my heart all at once as soon as I heard her name. I chuckled out.

"Don't worry Queen; she will come in a while. Now let me finish breakfast." I said.

Anvitha hit on my head and laughed.

After about half an hour, Shravan and his family arrived in their lavish car. Anvitha ran into kitchen, I followed her. Pushpa aunty and uncle rushed out to welcome them. I started bantering Anvitha, she blushed over and over.

When Shravan came in, I went out to living hall, we shook our hands. Shravan wished me back. There were five people with Shravan. I didn't know who were who. All took their seats on a huge sofa at living room.

I got a call from Apoorva. I came out and picked it up.

"Roshan, where are you?" Apoorva sounded anxious.

"Queen's place, why? What's wrong Apoorva?"

"Roshan come to Ooty main hospital right now." Apoorva said and hung up.

I was worried; I took my bike and rode to the hospital. Apoorva stood out waiting for me. I looked her from top till end but she was all right. Apoorva held my hand and took me into the ward. I found Jasmine sleeping on a bed. She was asleep. I was absolutely dismayed. I rushed near the bed and collapsed beside Jasmine. I begged Apoorva to say me what has happened. Apoorva came near me and brought me up. She took me out of ward and made me sit on a chair. She caressed my hair.

"Jasmine had a minor heart attack, when I called your landline to speak to you, Jasmine received it, she sounded strange and panicked; she asked me for help. I hurried to your home and brought her to hospital soon, but now there is nothing to worry about it Roshan, she is alright." Apoorva said and cupped my face.

I felt relaxed.

"Thank you Apoorva. But are you sure? Is she out of danger now?" I ensured it with Apoorva.

She gave me a nod. Apoorva made an eye contact with me. We looked into each other's eyes. I observed a sparkle in her eyes, which eagerly waited to get lost in my eyes. I was madly in love with her and I found the same feeling reciprocated from her.

Doctor interpreted us and said we can take Jasmine back home. We broke our eye contact and smiled at him. Jasmine was super fine when I took her back home. I made her sleep on bed and told her to rest. I came out of her room.

I got a knock on the door. I went up and opened it.

"Teddy…just now Apoorva said me that Jasmine was hospitalized. How is Jasmine now?" Anvitha said and hurried into Jasmine's room.

¥ ¥ ¥

"How was interview Roshan?" Jasmine asked when I was getting downstairs to dinner.

"It was good." I said taking my chair in dining table.

"It will be amazing if you get a job right?" Jasmine said with dazzled eyes.

I smiled at her.

"You should be thankful to Apoorva for this. Present her something." Jasmine said serving chapathi to me.

We started eating dinner.

"I don't think she's that kind of a girl who expects returns to her contributions." I said in confidence.

Jasmine shook. I asked what

"Being a woman I'm telling you, girls expectations are out of boys imaginations." She said and smiled.

I didn't understand. I ignored it and I continued my dinner. And then I remembered the advice of Anvitha's father so I decided to ask about Jasmine's past.

"Jasmine shall I ask you something?" I said looking at her.

"Sure." She uuld pouring water to her glass.

"Why you lived alone before adopting me? Why you adopted me? And do you have relatives?" I inquired about her.

"Huh today you felt like knowing about your mom?" Jasmine asked in curt.

"I was lost in your love and care which didn't reminded me to know about you Jasmine." I said in poignancy.

Jasmine gasped.

She brought an old photograph from her room and gave it to me. I looked at it.

"That is my husband Mr. Martin Morris. He is no more." She said pointing to the man in the picture.

I looked at him, he looked gentle.

"And that is my son Vincent Morris, he is in Spain but for me he is dead." Jasmine lost her temper.

I looked at Jasmine. Her eyes were red.

"We didn't live together for a long time. We looked after Vincent very well but he grew up to be a fraud. I hate people who cheat others, in that case how can I see my own son cheating others? In his 14 years of age he was caught smuggling, when I said him to stop all these, he blackmailed me that he would bitch about my character with my husband, That's it, I had my first heart attack then, after this I left Spain and came to Ooty." Jasmine said closing her eyes.

"Why did you adopt me?" I scrutinized Jasmine.

"I wanted to bring up a child as human not as a monster. That is why I adopted you and I always looked after you like my own son." Jasmine said and burst into tears.

I went near her and I held her shoulders. Jasmine's hands trembled. Since she already had heart attack once, I didn't wanted to stir her emotions anymore.

"You brought me up in such a way that I never felt I was an orphan Jasmine. I've been blessed to get you. I've got a real mother's love and care. I promise I won't bring up this topic again. Am sorry for making you cry Jasmine" I apologized her.

She wiped her tears. I consoled her. She stood up and went to her room.

¥ ¥ ¥

"I was not selected Apoorva." I said dampened.

"It's okay Roshan; we will try with other companies in Ooty." Apoorva said uprising me.

I nodded.

"Don't worry; if it is required I'll help you in preparing for your interview." Apoorva said.

Anvitha headed us holding a heavy handbag.

"Hi Teddy" Anvitha said and stowed her handbag on table.

"Hi Queen." I wished and smiled at her.

Anvitha embraced Apoorva.

"Anvitha what's in this bag?" Apoorva asked her.

"Invitations" Anvitha said and looked around.

"What invitations?" I asked Anvitha muddled.

"My engagement's" Anvitha said in rosy cheeks.

"Wow… Anvitha…" Apoorva said rubbing Anvitha's shoulder,

I winked at Anvitha.

All of us broke into laughter.

"Where is Shyam mama?" Anvitha stopped laughing and asked.

"Might be in" Apoorva said peeping inside tea house.

"Why?" I inquired Anvitha.

"To invite him to my engagement" Anvitha said and took an invitation out.

"Idiot, invite me first." I said pulling the invitation towards me.

"Hey… give it back." Anvitha snatched it from me and said- "I won't invite you, it's your responsibility to be present at my engagement, without invitation."

Apoorva laughed at us.

"It applies for you as well." Anvitha said turning to Apoorva.

Apoorva zipped her mouth and gave her an Indian headshake. Shyam mama came near and smiled at us.

"Hi mama, please do come to my engagement." Anvitha said and handed him invitation.

I looked at the lavish invitation. It was maroon in color and had Shravan's and Anvitha's picture in either ends.

"Thank you for inviting me Anvitha." Shyam mama said proudly for being invited for such a lavish function.

Anvitha smiled at him. Shyam mama went in and brought us tea. Apoorva went back to newspaper and marked vacancy ads which suit me.

"Apoorva is helping a lot to find you a job Teddy." Anvitha said keeping back denude tea cup.

"It's my duty." Apoorva blurted and bit her tongue.

Apoorva and I exchanged smiles. Anvitha observed us.

"Ok Apoorva I'll see you and bye Teddy take care." Anvitha said pulling my cheeks and left.

Apoorva was into newspaper. I sat gazing Apoorva; there was a ray of happiness in me.

¥ ¥ ¥

"For whom are you packing this gift Apoorva?" Ramesh uncle asked Apoorva savoring tea.

"For a newly married couple" Apoorva said cheekily.

"Where are you going?"

"Am going for a wedding with Roshan" Apoorva said writing her name on gift.

"Do you know the couple?"

"No…" Apoorva said laughing.

"Then why are you attending this wedding?"

"But I know Roshan very well." Apoorva said, stood up and texted me.

I texted back Apoorva to come out Apoorva came out in search of me. She held gift in her hand, she came near me.

"Where is your bike Roshan?"

"Can we go in your vehicle today?" I asked Apoorva.

"Yeah… we can and where is the marriage held?" Apoorva asked and smiled.

"St. Stephens church."

"Is it a Christian marriage?"

I nodded. I started vehicle, Apoorva sat behind me and she held my shoulder through-out our ride. We reached church in ten minutes and walked into the church.

"Roshan isn't she bride." Apoorva shouted jumping.

"Yes Apoorva." I said holding her hand, since she lost her grip while jumping.

Pastor entered the hall and everyone stood up and wished him. He asked all of us to take our seats back.

"There will be a marriage held in this church between James and Jessie. Does anyone here want to oppose the marriage?" Pastor announced.

The whole church fell silent. Pastor waited for five minutes and said- "Thank you for your co-operation."

The marriage ceremony started.

James and Jessie went up to Pastor and stood in front of him.

"James do you accept Jessie as your wife?" Pastor asked looking at groom.

"I'm James and I accept Jessie as my wife for this life. Thank you." James said.

"Jessie do you accept James as your husband?" Pastor asked turning to bride.

"I'm Jessie and I accept James as my husband." Jessie said and hung her face in shy.

Apoorva espied each and every bit of the ceremony. Marriage ended after James and Jessie exchanged their rings. Everyone surrounded to congratulate them and to take part of cake cut.

"Damn it, Apoorva I didn't bring gift." I said and held my forehead.

"Don't worry Roshan, I've brought it." Apoorva said and wrote my name after her name on the gift.

"So how does 'Apoorva Roshan' sounds?" she asked.

"I loved it, it's simply perfect." I said delighted.

Apoorva blushed. Apoorva and I went near James and Jessie; we wished them and handed over the gift. They received it and thanked us. James looked at the names in gift.

"Roshan, you have got a beautiful girlfriend." James said while we were walking back.

I turned behind to see him. Apoorva was put on cloud nine; I was euphoric listening to it. We smiled at him and walked into dining hall.

"One day even you will get married here right." Apoorva said, while we were walking to buffet.

"May be" I said.

"With a Christian girl huh?" Apoorva asked worried.

"No, with a Kannada girl" I said squinting Apoorva.

Apoorva's face turned happy and she held my elbow.

"Am eagerly waiting to wear bridal dress Roshan" Apoorva said gazing me.

Both of us felt pleasant. We served food ourselves and sat on a table.

"Roshan, why didn't you take chocolate cake?" Apoorva asked puzzled.

"I hate chocolate cake Apoorva." I said scrunching face.

Apoorva removed chocolate cake from her plate.

"What happened Apoorva?" I asked confused.

"I hate chocolate cake too." She said.

"Why?"

"Because I just found out someone I love, hate it too." Apoorva said in a cute smile.

I felt colors in my life after hearing it.

¥ ¥ ¥

"No Apoorva this is not happening. This is the fourth time am failing the interview." I said dejected.

"It's okay Roshan, don't lose hopes. Keep trying." Apoorva said and searched for that day's newspaper in tea house.

"No. I can do nothing." I said down in mouth.

"Don't get on my nervous Teddy." Anvitha said provoked by my talk.

"I just can't do this Queen."

"Just give it a last try Roshan." Apoorva requested.

"She is right Teddy, for our sakes." Anvitha requested me too.

I nodded. Anvitha ordered teas.

"Roshan there is an interview in two weeks at Mysore road, Ooty; for cost controller job." Apoorva said confirming from newspaper.

"At least get well prepared for this one Teddy, am worried for you." Anvitha said sleeping on my shoulder.

"Ok" I said passing tea to Apoorva.

"Teddy will you come with me, to see papa?" Anvitha said sipping tea.

"Why today?" I asked.

"It had been long time." Anvitha said.

"Am not in mood Queen, you carry on with it." I said playing around tea cup.

"Ok then I'll leave bye." Anvitha waved us.

We waved back her.

"Roshan please understand I want you to be a complete man." Apoorva said in concerned tone.

"Sure Apoorva." I said and smiled.

¥ ¥ ¥

"What's happening between you and Apoorva?" Jasmine asked me, while we ate dinner.

"What?" I was shocked.

Jasmine repeated her question.

"What do you mean by what's happening between us?" I asked avid.

"Don't act Roshan; I've come across your age." Jasmine said and served me onion curry.

I hung my head.

"So are you in love?" Jasmine questioned me.

I thought for a while, wondering either truth or a lie would go better. I decided to go with truth.

"Yes, we are in love." I admitted.

Jasmine's face lit up in delight.

"But how can it be possible? She is a Kannada girl; it's quite hard for her to get into a Christian family." Jasmine said glancing to the Jesus sculpture in the living room.

"It doesn't bother us Jasmine. We are genuinely in love with each others."

"Ok, so who expressed love first?" Jasmine was curious.

"Both of us know that we are in love with each other very much. There is no necessity to show it off." I said.

"There is no necessity of show off but expressing is important Roshan." Jasmine advised me.

I drank water from my glass.

"We express it every day." I said myself.

Jasmine refilled my glass. We remained silent for ten minutes.

"So what are her demands?" Jasmine started again.

"What demands?" I asked bewildered.

"I mean, what she wants you to be like?" Jasmine explained.

"Yeah… she wants me to be a complete man in all aspects, that she says me often." I said.

We finished our dinner. I went to washbowl.

"How do you know about girl's demands?" I asked washing my hands.

"I did the same, when I was in your age." Jasmine said blushing.

I wanted to drag that topic, since I had promised her not to speak about her family. I gave her a simple smile and went upstairs and reached room.

¥ ¥ ¥

"You are really strong in business and law Mr. Roshan; we don't think you can fit this job. Anyhow thank you for investing your time on our interview." The H.R said on phone.

"It's my pleasure sir." I said and hung my phone.

Apoorva called me after an hour. I felt ashamed to tell her that I flunked an interview again. I didn't receive her call. Apoorva called me repeatedly. I throwed my phone aside and I laid on my bed. I thought about my continuous failures. I was fazed.

After about twenty minutes, there was a knock on my door. I thought Jasmine had returned from church but I was startled to see Apoorva.

"What have you thought of yourself?" Apoorva glared at me as soon as she entered my room.

"Now what's wrong?" I said dejected.

"Why you didn't take my call?" Apoorva uplifted her voice.

"I should have received it to say you I've failed again right." I said and looked aside.

On the other hand I was happy to see my girl, in my room.

"That's okay Roshan; we do education to earn knowledge. We necessarily don't have to take it as our profession." Apoorva said and placed her hand on my shoulder.

I had a high voltage sensation since we were all alone in a lonely evening.

"If you don't get a job think of other virtues that you have to stand up in life." Apoorva said and sat across my bed.

"So what are you suggesting me?" I asked.

"To consider your pencil sketch art seriously, it will take you high."

"It's merely my hobby. I don't know to take it professionally." I said and shook.

"Make your heart Roshan. Come on you can do this. There is a state level pencil sketch competition next month in Ooty. You should participate in it." Apoorva said showing me a column in Moonlight mails newspaper.

Cool breeze from window hit our faces. Apoorva brushed back her hairs which fell on her eyes. Her fair cheeks, cute face and silky hairs seduced me. I shut my eyes and controlled it. I ignored the news paper.

"Will you participate in it Roshan?" Apoorva asked.

"How can I Apoorva. Like you know, till today I've never completed any sketches fully"

"Keep practicing it Roshan. Nothing is impossible." She said in winsome voice.

"Apoorva can I ask you something"

"Sure."

"If you don't mind, shall I sketch you?"

"Me???" Apoorva said with a surprised smile.

I nodded.

"Okay but will you complete my sketch at least?" Apoorva said brushing back her hairs.

I restrained myself again.

"I'll try." I said.

I brought pencil, a drawing sheet and an eraser. I adjusted the cardboard and sheet. I asked Apoorva to stand in front of me. She stood in front of me and rested against wall. I rolled my eyes on each a bit of her face. I was taken away for her charm. I felt like I had never seen anything gorgeous than her. I felt like I've got the prettiest girl on this earth. She blinked her eyes.

I gulped and held pencil. I started with those angelic eyes. We were silent. A bland light touched her lips by the time I almost completed the sketch. She licked her lips and moistened it. I had a gust deep inside me. Apoorva raised her eyebrows. I shook my head and went back to sketch. I completed the sketch except the lower lip part. Apoorva leaned towards my face.

"Roshan don't you like being a complete man?" Apoorva asked peeping to my sketch.

When she brought her face near mine, I was completely seduced for her fragrance.

"Yes but how much ever I tried, I couldn't complete it." I admitted my weakness.

I rubbed my finger on the lip portion on drawing sheet, not knowing the way to complete it.

"Rather than rubbing it in finger, touch it with the pencil Mr. Artist." Apoorva said and blushed.

I dropped cardboard and pencil down, I stood up and pushed her gently against wall. I moved my face slowly towards hers. I thought it gives her the option to turn aside, if she is uncomfortable. Apoorva looked into my eyes; she closed her eyes when our nose touched. I tilted my head sideway; I touched my lips on hers. She shivered suddenly and took in deep breath. I cupped her face from one hand, slowly stroked her cheek from my thumb and I held her waist from my other hand, Apoorva sighed. I took her lower lip in between mine. I was kind and gentle; she was forgiving and kept coming back. She stopped it for a while. Apoorva opened her eyes suddenly. She pushed me away, I fell on bed.

"Roshan this is wrong." She said.

Apoorva sobbed and ran out of my room.

¥ ¥ ¥

When you are truly in love with a person, it is difficult to stay not speaking to them even for a day. Next morning as soon as I woke up, I called Apoorva. She didn't take my call. I knew it's hard to bring Apoorva over the last evening. But it was tough for me to be unspoken. I kept calling her over and over but she didn't receive it at all. One can avoid a call but not a message.

Me: I'm sorry Apoorva. Please forgive me for yesterday. But don't avoid me like this.

I texted her, but I didn't get any answer.

Me: Please reply me Apoorva.

After about twenty minutes, there was a reply from her.

Apoorva: why did you kiss me Roshan? Am not like other girls. It's not so casual for me.

Me: It's my mistake. Forgive me Apoorva; it all happened out of my senses.

Apoorva: Don't fool me Roshan.

I sent her a crying smiley within a second. She sent me two. Then I thought girls are clever.

Me: Please meet me in the evening.

Apoorva: No Roshan, I can't.

Me: Please Apoorva I need to see you, please…

There was no reply for five minutes.

Me: don't say me no Apoorva please.

I messaged her again.

Apoorva: Okay, but not in tea house.

Me: Fine, we will meet at Moonlight lamp.

That evening I waited for Apoorva under Moonlight lamp. I sat on one of the benches. Half an hour later Apoorva arrived on her vehicle. She put on a sad face while walking to me. She came and sat a bit far from me on the same bench and looked away from me.

Her hairs fell on her eyes again and again but she didn't brush it back this time. I looked aside and shook my head.

"Am sorry Apoorva" I said turning to her.

She didn't look at me, she kept gazing aside.

"Apoorva am sorry, don't hurt me now." My eyes were about to tear when I said it.

"It's not easy to resist this, being a Kannada girl Roshan." She said in anger.

"I can't live without you Apoorva." I cried like a kid in front of her.

"Don't behave like I don't have any feelings on you Roshan, I just can't imagine my life without you in it. But I have not learned living in a space where in, I move closely with a guy but not married to him. You should know what feelings I carry for you, when I've compromised my roots for you." Apoorva said almost breaking to cry.

I held her palm on bench, she didn't reject. I kept my hand around her shoulder. Apoorva increased sobbing.

"Am sorry, am sorry Apoorva." I said in trembling voice.

She held my shirt and buried her face in my chest. I caressed her hair.

"At least be serious from now Roshan." Apoorva cheered.

"Okay Apoorva… calm down." I consoled her.

¥ ¥ ¥

"Don't get low Ramesh; you better appoint other faculty to that school." Radha aunty said to her husband.

"No one are coming forward to go there Radha." Ramesh uncle gasped and continued-"if we won't get any one now, we can't help closing down the school."

"Shall I speak to Apoorva about this?" Radha aunty asked uncle.

"What can Apoorva do?" Ramesh uncle said resting his head on sofa.

"If everything goes well, we can send Apoorva there to be a teacher." Radha aunty said making her heart strong.

"What are you saying Radha? You know the situation there right it's getting worse day by day. Religious conflicts have taken hundreds of lives already, am scared to send our daughter there." Uncle said in apathy.

"How will others send their children Ramesh? This school is important for us; we should retain it at any cost." Radha aunty persuaded uncle.

"Okay let's see what Apoorva will say." Ramesh uncle said and stood up.

Apoorva went home a bit late that evening.

"Apoorva…" Radha aunty called out.

"What Amma." Apoorva said and looked at uncle.

"We need to speak to you Apoorva" Radha aunty said looking at uncle.

Uncle went near Apoorva.

"What Appa? Why are you upset? What's happening?" Apoorva asked and held uncle's hand.

Uncle put his hand around Apoorva's shoulder and walked to sofa, aunty followed them. Uncle explained the entire problem to Apoorva.

"No Appa, I can't leave Ooty and go anywhere." Apoorva said in blues.

"This school is important for us Apoorva." Aunty interpreted.

"Living in Ooty is equally important for me Amma. I can't leave Roshan alone and go anywhere." Apoorva said dissented.

"Then I don't have any other way left. I should close down the school." Uncle said in agony.

"We will see where life takes us Appa." Apoorva said and went upstairs with a doleful look on her face.

¥ ¥ ¥

"Hi Roshan" Apoorva wished me on phone.

"Hi Apoorva" I wished her back.

"Come to tea house, I need to see you." Apoorva said.

"Am practicing sketch Apoorva, we will meet in the evening."

"No Roshan, you are meeting me now in tea house, that's it." Apoorva said and hung up.

"Damn." I said gasping.

Apoorva went to tea house in her vehicle and sat on a chair alone under a bower. It was a bright morning and Moonlight streets shone for a mollifying sun rays. Apoorva waited for me in tea house. Shyam mama brought tea and handed it to Apoorva. Apoorva took it.

"Am waiting for Roshan mama, you should have brought it after he drop in." Apoorva said and stared 4th cross expecting my arrival.

"Apoorva can I ask you something?" Shyam mama asked Apoorva utterly deadpan.

"Sure." Apoorva said and smiled.

She still held tea cup but didn't sip it.

"What's new between you and Roshan? Am seeing you together quite often now a days."

Apoorva blushed. Her tiny eyes lit up a joyous glint.

"Apoorva… am speaking to you." Shyam mama interrupted.

Apoorva came back.

"Yes mama, we are in love." Apoorva said shyly.

"Love? Is it only you or even Roshan loves you?" Shyam mama asked deliberated.

"What are you saying? I said both of us are in love with each other." Apoorva clarified.

Shyam mama gave a mock smile and said-"Chandan will love you and you love someone else and let that person deceive you."

Anvitha walked to Tea House and observed unusual conversation between Shyam mama and Apoorva from far.

"What rubbish? Chandan is a very good friend of mine. I've never felt that way with him mama." Apoorva strived to utter words.

"Chandan loved you but Roshan fooled him saying he loved you before Chandan. Like you know, Chandan is a sensitive boy, to come out of the tort of being in love with his best friend's girl, he left Ooty. Everything around you is cheating Apoorva. Roshan is a playboy, moreover he is not serious in his life, and in this case, how can you expect to consider you seriously in his life?

He doesn't have consistency to be a one girl's man Apoorva. I advised him to stop all this before things could get any serious but he didn't seem like caring me. Am saying you this because I know you are a delicate kid, I can't see you broken and hurt. Wake up Apoorva." Shyam mama explained.

Apoorva was blindfolded, she felt dark all around her though it was a bright sunny day. She was stunned; she stepped a bit back and held table for her grip.

"Shyam anna" A customer called out loudly.

Shyam mama stared Apoorva for a while and went back to his customers.

Tears filled Apoorva's eyes and rolled down her cheeks. Apoorva throwed tea cup away and it broke apart. Shyam mama looked back and noticed broken tea cup but he went in without reacting. She lost strength to wipe off her tears. She rushed to her vehicle and went off, when Anvitha neared Tea House. Anvitha shouted her name but Apoorva didn't stop. Anvitha went near Shyam Mama to inquire about Apoorva's unusual behavior.

I went to tea house an hour late and sat on a chair waiting for Apoorva. I was happy to meet Apoorva that day. I took out my phone and called Apoorva but I was offended to hear the tone which said switched off.

Shyam mama came near me. I stood up and wished him. He gave me a teasing smile. I felt super irritated to digest his smiles. I felt uneasy since Apoorva's phone was switched off.

"Whom are you searching so much?" Shyam mama asked though he knew the fact.

"Did you see Apoorva around?" I inquired.

"Yes, she left an hour back."

"Okay." I said and turned back to leave.

"I'm sorry" Shyam mama apologized.

"Why are you sorry?" I asked perplexed.

"You will get to know soon." He said and went in.

Seeing Apoorva seemed more important for me than his apology. So I didn't react to it but I felt something is wrong that day. I nodded and left tea house.

¥ ¥ ¥

Though I did well in the state level sketch competition, I felt incompleteness. My sketch was put under top ten the best sketches but I didn't win the competition. In addition to that Apoorva's sudden egression of Ooty dashed me into pieces and I was all torn up. I was ruffled.

An hour back home ride in a sunny afternoon made me tired. I entered home and called out for Jasmine. No one replied, I thought Jasmine has gone out. I searched everywhere but I didn't find her. I shouted her name repeatedly and entered her room. Jasmine was asleep. I sighed and went near her.

"Jasmine" I called softly.

She didn't react.

"I didn't win the competition Jasmine." I said in a pale tone.

Jasmine did not wake up.

I stared her for a while and I churned her. Her body was stiffened. She neither didn't replied me nor responded for my churn, I was scared. When I stretched my hand forth to check her breathe, my hand shivered. When I didn't felt her breathing, I confirmed her death. I felt deep pain inside which brought tears in my eyes. I closed my eyes and covered my face.

I realized the real meaning of the word orphan that day. I didn't know what to do; I took my phone and ringed Anvitha.

That evening, Jasmine was kept in coffin and it was filled with garlands. Anvitha held my hand grieving over Jasmine's death. Shyam mama stood far regretting his mistakes. Papa patted my back consoling me.

"Roshan" Anvitha's father called me.

"Yes uncle." I said in crestfallen voice.

"Do you know Vincent?" he inquired.

"Yes… Jasmine's son, she said me about him once but I don't know much about her family." I said, though tears rolled down.

"It's okay Roshan. Listen we can't wait for Vincent because we don't know where he is. So we will continue the burial." He said and stepped a bit back.

I nodded.

Anvitha tightened her hold on my hand and screamed in grief.

Radha and Pushpa aunty sobbed.

Anvitha's father stood behind me throughout the funeral. I returned back home, my home looked as empty as me. Anvitha stayed with me for a week after Jasmine's death. I said Anvitha about my love; that is when Anvitha said me the incident that happened in Tea House the other day.

Anvitha's father handed me Jasmine's will, which said the entire property of Jasmine belongs to me. I shed tears when I received it. That was a time when I started living again with my old orphanage friend, Jesus sculpture.

¥ ¥ ¥

"Am sorry Roshan" Oshini said holding my hands.

Her eyes were wet.

"I've become real orphan after Jasmine's death." I said rubbing my moistened eyes.

"Did you meet Chandan again?"

"No, I didn't meet him again." I said.

"Did he return to Ooty on Jasmine's death?"

"That day none of us had his contact to inform him about her death." I said.

"Then where is Chandan now?" She asked me in eager.

"Still in Mysore, He has re-opened our orphanage with the help of Shravan Rao and he is the administrator of the orphanage now" I said.

"Wow… he is a nice man." Oshini said inspired.

"Logically Chandan has become the hero." I said and continued-"Especially in someone's mind."

Oshini blushed and asked-"So how do you know about Chandan now."

"Anvitha said me, only after her engagement she got to know that Chandan worked with Shravan for few months." I said.

"How you said me the things happened in your absence in the story?" Oshini asked.

"Apoorva said me some and Anvitha told me the rest." I said.

"Oh… okay and when is Anvitha's Marriage?" Oshini inquired.

"Next week and she has shifted to Mysore." I said and smiled.

"What about Moonlight streets then?" Oshini asked addled.

"Moonlight streets are empty now. It has lost its shine."

Oshini looked sad as soon as she heard it. Her eyebrows and eyes dragged my attention. We were silent for minutes. Oshini placed her hand on my shoulder. Train cut down speed and stood in the final station. I lifted my head. People hurried towards our train. I noticed a yellow wide board called "New Delhi."

"This is my story." I said and stood up.

Oshini hung her face nodding, hot sunrays touched her face.

"Get up Oshini, we should get down." I said taking my luggage out.

"I never knew Delhi is so near to Ooty!" Oshini said and stood up.

"What do you mean?" I gave her a weird look.

"I can't take the fact that we are departing." Oshini said staring me.

We walked near the door, Oshini held my pencil sketch in her left hand. I was scared to get down. Delhi railway station was crowded unlike our Moonlight streets.

I helped Oshini to get down and I stepped down the train. We smiled at each other. I didn't find reason for being friend with her so soon. We walked to the less crowded part of the station. I focused my look on the big wall clock of the station and said myself it was 6:30pm.

"Roshan can we have tea together?" Oshini requested.

I agreed to her with a smile. We walked out of the station and went to a tea shop. Oshini ordered two teas. We sat on a corner table.

"I want to meet Chandan once." Oshini expressed her desire.

I smiled at her raising my eyebrows.

"You know, I liked him." I observed a sparkle in her face, when Oshini said it.

"I know." I said her.

"How?" Oshini asked and made her eyes wide.

"Girls like innocence than everything else."

"You are a great person too Roshan." Oshini said and smiled.

"Oh… Really?" I asked, smiling back.

"Yeah… believe me." Oshini said and held my hands.

We were served with two teas. We started savoring it.

"Don't worry you will certainly get your girl." Oshini said and comforted me.

I gave her a satisfied smile.

"Do you still love her truly?"

"I love her all my life." I said.

"Is Apoorva that beautiful? I should see her once." Oshini said and placed back her empty cup on table.

"You have seen her." I said shocking her.

"What? Where Roshan?" Oshini asked surprised.

"In the sketch in your bag" I said pointing to her bag.

Oshini was gratified and was pleasantly surprised.

"Roshan was it Apoorva? She looks like a dol. I thought this sketch was your imagination." Oshini said mesmerized.

I smiled and we walked out of the tea shop.

"I need your autograph on this sketch Roshan." Oshini said giving me the sketch. I signed it at the end and returned her the pen.

"What else do you want?" I asked Oshini to accomplish it.

"Yes, a cup of green tea with all five of you in Moonlight streets." Oshini said and winked.

"We will see, may be, very soon," I said and extended my hand.

We shook our hands and Oshini gave me a hug. I came out of her arms after a while and I turned back and we walked opposite to each other.

"Roshan..." I heard Oshini calling me.

I turned back again.

"I forgot to ask you something very important." Oshini shouted from a bit far from me.

"Ask me what." I shouted back.

"Where is Apoorva now?"

"Kulu-Manali" I said.

She raised her thumb and wished me good lucks. I smiled, waved her bye and we walked apart. I reached Delhi suburban bus stand in an hour and I felt a bit relieved. Sun was about to set and it was chilly. The entire bus stand was crowded and had noise pollution.

I searched for Manali platform. When I reached there, I noticed a red bus. I walked up to the conductor. He chewed pan and he had red tongue.

"Excuse me sir." I asked him.

He focused to me.

"Manali bus?" I asked.

He pointed me the same red bus. I thanked him and I boarded the bus. The bus was filled with lots of passengers; still I managed to take a window seat. The driver gave an annoying continuous horn indicating the departure. All passengers were comfortable except me. I was uncomfortable in the absence of Oshini Dhavanth.

Bus started and moved. I closed my eyes and gasped out. I opened my eyes and looked out from window. I saw a girl in pink salwar from her back. I put out my head from window to confirm if it was Oshini. But when bus moved forth, I was disappointed, it was not her. I rested my head on seat and closed my eyes. I sunk in my deep thoughts.

"Why Oshini liked Chandan over me? Am I cheap or am I a bummer? No, I don't think Chandan is so great like she has thought. I know him well; I've seen him from our childhood. I would have accepted it, if Anvitha had told me, but how can Oshini decide his personality? She has not even seen him once. I think Oshini is impressed by his gentleman attitude. Yes, her choice is great. Chandan is a gentleman and Oshini??? She is a pretty, bubbly and active girl. Unlike poles always attract each others. In the matter of a day Oshini has become one of the important people in my life."

My shoulder was held by someone. I opened my eyes suddenly.

"Sir Ticket" conductor said taking back his hand. I gave him money and took my ticket. Conductor successfully put a final dot for all my random meaningless thoughts. An aged Tibetan sat beside me. I looked at him, he smiled me. I smiled back him.

"Excuse me." I asked the Tibetan.

He turned to me.

"How long does it take to reach Manali?" I asked him.

"About ten hours from here. We will reach there by tomorrow around six in the morning." He explained gesturing his hands.

"Thank you." I said him.

Full moon was up in the sky already. I felt extremely cold; I rubbed my palms and shut the window.

"This bus will not go inside Manali town. You should walk about five kilometers to reach Manali from there." He gave me the extra information.

"Okay… thank you." I thanked him again.

We didn't speak again. After about half an hour he dozed off. I closed my eyes resting against seat, Apoorva's cute face flashed. I opened my eyes and started watching roads from window.

¥ ¥ ¥

I woke up for conductor's harsh yelling. When I opened my eyes, I felt severe cold but I was used to that kind of a climate and it didn't bother me much. I looked out of window. I saw an open green grass land, tall green trees, green mountains and tea plantations; I saw sheep and cows raised on the other side. I felt like I was driven to a never ending green land.

"Manali?" I asked conductor.

He shouted at me to get down.

I took out my luggage and got down of bus. I looked all around; I didn't find a single habitat. I walked for some time and found a shepherd near a small pond. I adjusted my bag and walked near him.

"Where is Manali?" I asked him.

"This is outskirts of Manali. You should walk for another three kilometers to reach Manali village." He said and pointed me the way to village.

I thanked him and walked on the way he suggested

Morning's cold breeze freshened my face and huge fog made roads fuzzy. I walked by a small stream, it looked outstandingly beautiful. The greenery all around gave me refreshment after a long journey. After an hour of walking, I noticed a cowherd resting beneath the tree. I went near him and asked for Manali.

"This is Manali." He said.

The instancy to see Apoorva increased each second. I was elated and was exalted.

"Thanks." I said and turned back to leave.

"But be careful, Manali has been declared as a sensitive place now." He advised in anxiety.

"What? What do you mean?" I asked in confusion.

"Yes, it is religious disputes in Manali. By God's grace from last two days it has slightly been under control. But conflicts may arise any time, you better go back." He explained me.

"It's okay... and do you know this address?" I asked him showing a slip, which Anvitha gave me.

"I don't know if this is correct address or not, I got it from Apoorva's parents but if your presence disturbs her, please don't go Roshan." I remembered Anvitha's advice, when I took out the slip.

He gave me a blank look. I understood it, so I kept back the slip in my pocket.

"Don't risk your life, just go back and come when things are fine in village." He warned me.

"No, this is important for me." I said and walked towards village.

"Is it worth your life?" He shouted caring me.

"Worth hundreds of its kind" I said and ran towards the village.

I entered Manali village exactly at 8:30am. I hardly found people out. I saw some posters, who looked like some local politicians in the poster and they were stained from cow-dung and few posters were garlanded by slippers in dishonor. I walked forth, watching all these. I noticed a small provision store and a man in it.

I gasped and ran to him.

"Sir" I called him.

"Yes." He said and looked at me.

"Do you know this address?" I asked and passed him the slip.

He took it and read it.

"No… this is wrong address sir." He said and gave back me the slip.

"Are you sure?" I asked him worried.

"I've been staying in Manali since thirty years. I know each and every corners of this village but I've not come across this address till now. I promise you this is fake address." He said and moved to his customers.

I was completely chopped and broken. I was not scared of trying again but I was sick of failures in my life. I walked forth aimless. I found a college boy next, believing to be a last try; I went near him and asked him the way to that address.

He shook his head before he could completely read it.

"I think this is a wrong address." He said and walked away.

I stood there for a minute pointless. I turned around and walked back the way I had come.

I walked as slow as possible in no heart to leave Manali. It was difficult to return to Moonlight streets without Apoorva. After about a couple of minutes walk in cold, I found a small school girl standing alone by road. She was upset. I went to her and stood beside her. She looked at me and hung her head down. She was dressed in white uniform and had school bag with her.

"What's your name?" I asked her in a polite tone.

"Shreya" She said in a small voice.

"What happened? Why are you Sad?" I inquired.

"I have missed my school bus." She said in sunken voice.

"What is the big deal?" I asked her.

"Grandy said Manali is unsafe for some days and am scared to walk alone until my school." She said and started sobbing.

I loved her innocence, she reminded me of Apoorva. I gave her a smile.

"Don't worry; I will take you to your school." I said.

"Promise?" Shreya asked in eager, stopping to sob suddenly.

"Yes." I assured.

Shreya smiled and took her school bag. She held my hand and we walked towards her school. I got a call; I took out my phone from my pocket. It was a call from an unknown number, I received it.

"Hi Roshan" A familiar voice wished me.

"Hello." I said in a dull voice.

"Did you meet Apoorva?" The voice said.

I realized it was Oshini.

"No Oshini, I've got wrong address." I said her dejected.

"Oh… Damn it." She said in sorrow.

"I've been defeated Oshini. I can never go back and make things all right." I said in trembling voice.

"Roshan don't be sad, nothing has come to an end. Give some time and wait till everything gets on right track. I think you need me now, we should speak!" Oshini bucked up me.

"Very much Oshini, I'll leave Manali in an hour and I want you to meet me today night in Delhi." I said.

"Sure Roshan."

"Okay Oshini." I said and she disconnected the call.

I wiped my tears. We reached Shreya's school. It was not a big school, it was an average school with a small play ground I observed plants in front of all classes.

"Okay Shreya get in. I will go now, bye." I said pushing her gently inside the school gates.

"No, come till my class room." She said and held my finger again.

"Why?" I asked.

"Today is my birthday so please come with me to celebrate it with my friends" Shreya requested.

"Okay." I said.

She took me near her class room.

"She is my teacher." Shreya said pointing to the lady in the class room.

That lady was busy writing something on black board. She finished it and turned back.

I was startled, when I saw her face.

It was Apoorva.

She was dressed in plain orange sari, her blouse ended full armed, she had tied her hairs lose, she wore a decent specks. It was first time ever I saw her in sari and she looked gorgeously beautiful. My heart beats rose up. I stood there as if I was in seventh heaven. I felt like I lived an hundred meaningful lives soon I saw her. I appeared strong and peppy.

I gave her a relieved breath.

Apoorva walked to us, looking at Shreya. Though she noticed me, she reacted like I was a stranger. She came near us.

"Apoorva…. Are you here? I searched whole of the Manali for you." I said slowly tired.

She didn't make an eye contact with me. She held Shreya's little hand to take her in.

"Apoorva answer me, why you didn't say me your departure from Moonlight streets?" I asked her a bit louder and on a serious note. All the children, in the class room, stared at us.

Apoorva stood in front of me in silence and looked aside.

"Am sorry, am sorry for everything that has happened. I want you back Apoorva, it's not easy being without you." I said and looked at her eyes.

"It's not easy being a cheat as well Roshan." Apoorva said in anger and focused her look on me.

It was tough to face her eyes. I looked aside. She shook her head and pulled Shreya, walking to class room.

"Apoorva listen, I can't live without you." I repeated I had low voice.

She turned to me.

"Just go away Roshan." Apoorva said in trembling voice.

"Apoorva don't hurt me over and again, I have already had enough. I can't resist sufferings anymore." I said looking tired.

Apoorva squint my face.

"Apoorva I've already lost Jasmine permanently." I said in stirred tone.

"Roshan!!! What happened?" Apoorva asked me anxious.

She looked into my eyes, her fuming face gradually turned to sympathetic face.

"I know it is none of your business. I have not come here to grieve over Jasmine's death." I said in moistened eyes.

Apoorva broke down. I removed my bag and took out her pencil sketch. Apoorva fixed her focus on my sketch.

"Am a complete man now Apoorva. I have won India's the best sketcher award for your sketch. This is your completed sketch. I have not come here to force you for anything. I have come here to give you this and to clear your blues on me." I said and offered her that sketch.

She declined it.

"Keep it, this sketch belongs to you." I offered her again.

"Nothing belongs to me." Apoorva replied.

"That's my dialogue, because it's me who has lost everyone and now am a real orphan." I said and took my bag up on my shoulders.

I wanted to confirm Apoorva that I wasn't a cheater.

"Apoorva remember that I had not cheated anyone. Everything that I had told you is true." I said.

"Then why you didn't say that Chandan loved me?" Apoorva asked giving me an immediate reaction.

I made my eyes wide.

"You faked your love. You deceived me to fool Chandan." Apoorva said while tears rolled down her eyes. She removed her specks and wiped her tears.

"Chandan had a crush on you. It was not love. I admit that I fooled Chandan saying that I loved you but never meant to hurt him. Chandan, knowing me from childhood could have compromised his sensitivity." I said and continued- "On the other end of spectrum you do not know the toughest war which was fought between my mind and heart when I lost Chandan and when I realized my feelings for you. I had an excruciating pain just because I loved you. It was not a cake walk decision for me to accept my proceeding with my love for you. Am not accusing you or angry on you Apoorva. I just want you all through my life. I have completed the sketch. But I'll never be complete without you." I said convincing her.

I noticed a sudden change in Apoorva's face. She was pink and I observed a guilt feeling in her face. I stood there for a while. I expected a reply from her but she didn't speak a word. I did not want to be rude to her. I sighed and turned back to leave.

Shreya held my hand. I looked at her, I went down to her and I pulled her cheeks, thanking her for showing me Apoorva unexpectedly.

"Uncle it's my birthday today." Shreya said me.

She opened her box and offered me a cake, but it was a chocolate cake.

"Happy birthday Shreya, but I hate chocolate cake." I wished her and gave her a kiss, declining chocolate cake.

Shreya's face was sunken and she offered the same cake to Apoorva and she smiled.

Apoorva hugged Shreya and wished her.

"Happy birthday Shreya but I hate Chocolate cake too." She blushed.

"Why madam" Shreya inquired, blinking her eyes innocently.

"Because the person I love hate it too." Apoorva said squinting at me and smiled.

I gave a winsome gasp.

"Finally I won her." I said to myself.

¥ ¥ ¥

EPILOGUE

I ran to her.

"Hi Roshan" She said with glowing eyes.

I smiled at her and we hugged.

I took her into the Tea House and we sat on the opposite chairs. We had another four empty chairs around our table. She smiled at me often and I knew she was enraptured.

"So how are you?" I asked her.

"Am fine Roshan and how are you?" She asked still smiling.

"Am fine" I said and returned her the smile. My phone rang to interrupt our conversation.

I received it and spoke for a minute. After a while Shyam Mama came down to take order.

"Hi Shyam mama" She wished him.

Shyam mama looked at her in response and gradually shifted his focus on me.

"Six green teas" I said and laughed.

Shyam mama went into tea house, both of us looked at each other and we broke into laughter.

"So where are others?" She eagerly asked.

I indexed my finger at street. A swift car stood in front of tea house. She turned her face to look out. And a person got down from it, He walked into tea house. He was dressed in blazer.

"Roshan… Isn't he Chandan?" She asked and her face instantly brightened.

I gave her a smiling nod.

"Wow!!!" She said and stood up.

Chandan came to our table and stood in front of me. I stood up. He gave me a hug. I hugged him back, terribly missing him. When we came out of each other's arms, we had wet eyes.

"I missed you." Chandan said and continued "I didn't know about Jasmine's death Roshan, am sorry for not being with you in your bad times." He rubbed his eyes.

I patted his back giving him a half smile.

"By the way, this is Oshini Dhavanth" I said to Chandan pointing her.

"Hi... Oshini" Chandan said and extended his hand.

"Hi Chandan, nice to meet you" Oshini said frantic.

"Nice to meet you too" Chandan said and they shook their hands.

Oshini's expression was cynical. Chandan sat beside me. Oshini didn't take her eyes off him. Soon we heard a car approaching and we looked out, while Oshini kept gazing at Chandan. Anvitha and Shravan got down. I shook Oshini gesturing her to look out.

Oshini noticed them.

"Anvitha and Shravan right" Oshini asked looking at Anvitha's outfit.

I nodded.

Anvitha ran to us and hugged me and Chandan. We hugged her back.

"Queen, this is Oshini." I said.

"Hi... Oshini am Anvitha Shravan." Anvitha said and hugged her.

"And that is Shravan." I said pointing at him.

Oshini and Shravan exchanged formal smiles. Before Anvitha could take her seat beside Shravan, we noticed Apoorva hurrying into tea house. She came to us and stood in front of Chandan. We all smiled at her.

"I think you are sitting in my place" Apoorva said to Chandan and blushed.

"Oh... Sorry Madam, the chair and the person sitting next to me belongs to you" Chandan said bantering Apoorva.

Apoorva laughed back. Apoorva hugged Oshini and Anvitha, she smiled at Shravan. Chandan stood up. Apoorva sat next to me. Since there was only one chair left beside Oshini.

Chandan sat beside to her.

Shyam mama brought us teas. We all took our cups.

I kept my hand around Apoorva. Anvitha and Shravan held their hands. Oshini and Chandan looked at each other.

"My desire has been accomplished Roshan." Oshini said, squinting Chandan.